SPREZZATURA

by

Tommy Dishman

TABLE OF CONTENTS

For Scott & Sarah

Note:

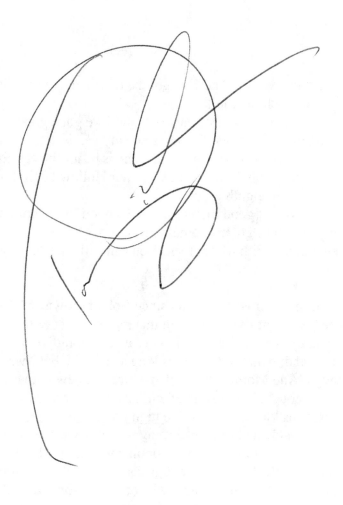

The Creek

I've got the cancer. And I've got the degenerative eye disease. And I ain't got much time left.

I'm eighty-eight years old, and I've got a great granddaughter writing this stuff down for me, since my hands don't work so good no more. Her name is Scarlet, and she is beautiful. It's for her English class. She's a junior at Squalor Hollow High. I, myself, only made it to the eighth grade.

I've got good memories, had a good life beholding to the Almighty; but I got me some regrets, too. My name is Clementine. Clementine Judith McLintock. You can call me Clemmy.

It's been seventy-three years since Robert drowned. That's seventy-three years that I've lived with this regret. Seventy-three years of fearing torment and damnation because I should've been holding on to his hand; which I did, for as long as I could, but I wasn't strong enough. And Momma knew it and Daddy knew it, that I wasn't strong enough, but they had their hands full: trying to make sure all seven of us kids made it to the high ground in time.

Daddy had to carry Jimmy—Jimbo, we called him—because he was born with water on the brain and couldn't fend for hisself. Jimbo was eleven or twelve, I guess. He was the oldest of us. And, Daddy, with his other hand, he had to pull Momma up that big hill. Momma was a healthy, stout old gal; you had to be, back then. Daddy was skinny as a reed; so you can imagine the struggle he had. Momma carried Annie, the baby, on her other arm. Randy held on to Momma's dress with one hand, and pulled me using his other. I pulled Marybeth and she pulled Robert. Robert pulled Ben. Don't ask me to recollect their precise ages. I can barely remember in what order everyone was born.

The rain didn't stop falling that spring. We lived in a single-story shack at the foot of Buncombe Mountain. Daddy was a logger—the best there ever was, folks used to say. And he was handsome too, despite being so skinny. He worked for his dad, until a tree fell on him, sending him to the Promised Land. Daddy found the body; had to dig half of it out, just to turn around and bury him all over again. Daddy became the big man at McLintock Logging then, running the show really well, despite being just twenty years of age or so. He made and repaired crosscut saws for other logging operations, too.

Momma's maiden name was Draymond. Draymond Logging was Daddy's biggest competitor. But I reckon that didn't stop them from falling in love. Or, more precisely, getting knocked up, I guess you could say. They loved music and to dance. When they were within arms' length of one another, you couldn't keep Hollis McLintock off of Janey Draymond, they used to say. Or vice versa, if you don't mind me being so uncultivated. Anyway, my Granddad Draymond helped Daddy build that shack before Jimbo was born.

Momma used to say that God gave mountain people like us special feet. She said our feet were different, allowing us to hike to the top of the steepest hill and run back down the other side of it quick as a cat. But I reckon God hisself couldn't have expected that much rain—the amount we got back in spring of forty-five. It came up on us one night, calm as a Hindu cow, and it stayed calm. Day after day after day, it stayed calm. No thunder, no big wind…just weeks of slow, steady rain.

We watched it fill the creek bed; we watched it sneak up to the front porch like an unwelcome Jee-hovah's Witness. We watched it start rolling in under the front door before Daddy even said we might have a problem on our hands. But he didn't do nothing about it. Mommy made us all pray that it wouldn't get no higher.

It got higher, alright.

We didn't have nice furniture; but what we did have, Momma stacked up so the water wouldn't ruin it. That only bought us some time. Then we got word that our old teacher at the one-room schoolhouse, mean old Miss Burkett, had called off classes until further notice. So there Momma was: one on the tit, one chair-bound, and five more crazy and hungry kids getting in trouble and playing in cold water slowly taking over her house; all while Daddy spent sun-up to sundown in the woods.

Our house sat on a lot of land, some ninety acres, give or take, so we didn't have neighbors close by; but we knew they were all leaving ahead of us because they all stopped and asked if we needed help packing up. Momma always told them no. Daddy was in the woods, so he couldn't say nothing. So we prayed, several times a day, that the rain would stop and the water would stop coming in. We didn't wear shoes in the house—hardly ever, actually—so that cold water rising inch-by-inch was bound to make us sick. Us kids had to share beds, which weren't really beds at all—more like bare mattresses; and these mattresses were on the floor and in every room. Early-on during the rain we, me and Randy, I mean, put the mattresses on tables or anything we could find to keep us out of the water that was rising slowly day after day. And we had to keep wheeling poor Jimbo about because the roof leaked constantly; and everywhere we put him, raindrops would find him. I guess that's irony: considering his condition and all. I hope that doesn't make me sound mean. Lord forgive me, if it does.

Well, one night I guess Daddy finally had enough of Momma's complaining, so he said the next morning, which was a Sunday, we would all head to high ground. 'Bout damn time, too; the water was so high in the house that it was up to Jimbo's chest whilst sitting in his chair. The lowlands in the county were completely flooded and the more we prayed the worse it got. We were the only family stupid enough to still be down there.

The night before we left, a Saturday night it was, a couple men on horseback came to the house. Completely soaked, Daddy asked them in; even though we couldn't offer any coffee or warm blankets that weren't already in use by us kids. They declined; said they were with the Squalor Hollow Rescue Squad. They wanted to take the youngest ones of us into the town, set them up with old Doc McInnis' family until the rest of us could join them. They said they would make as many trips as it took to get us all out, if we accepted their graciousness. They were kind—I remember it like it was yesterday. But Momma said her babies would stay beside her every night until the day they had families of their own. Daddy tried, if you want to call it that, to change her mind. He said the next day's climb to the top of Buncombe Mountain would be easier if Annie, Ben, and Robert went on ahead of us with those men. And he was right; but there was no changing Momma's mind. In her benevolence, she allowed one of the men to pack Jimbo's wheelchair back with them.

Something inside me said it was a mistake—that these men were sent like angels to help us. But Momma, for all her praying, didn't see it that way. And even after little Robert drowned, and all the way up to her own death, she never admitted to God or anybody that she was wrong. But all those damn Draymonds were that way.

Morning came and Momma stood in water waist-high, nursing Annie and giving us our Sunday School lesson while Daddy filled empty potato sacks with whatever food he could find that wasn't completely ruined by moisture. He had a wad of paper money that he split with Momma, in case the rain ruined what he stashed inside the zippered-pocket of his overalls. He gave each of us kids a silver dollar apiece; the ones he was saving for our birthdays. Even though I'm a February baby—the twelfth; same as Honest Abe Lincoln and that science man that said we came from monkeys—and he already gave me mine a couple months before, he gave me another one anyway. Daddy wasn't the brightest, as he would say, but he always tried to be fair.

I was sitting cross-legged Indian-style on a big oak table, Jimbo propped up against me, back-to-back when Momma finished her lesson and Daddy said it was time. I still had a bad feeling; and I could tell Daddy did too. I could just tell. The rain was still falling calmly when he snatched up Jimbo and threw him over his right shoulder. Normally before leaving the house Momma would ask us all if we needed to visit the outhouse; but, as nasty as it sounds, there was no point in it by then: we were all wading in our own filth. We all knew it, but none of us spoke about it.

The rain wasn't cold. Or maybe it was; we were just so used to it that it didn't bother us no more. We had our assignments, knowing who to hold on to when we started the climb up Buncombe, the tallest mountain in Squalor Hollow; which could have meant it was the tallest in the world, for all we knew. All I know is that when we were behind the house, and I looked up at it, this same mountain I'd seen all my life, mind you, it seemed to reach Heaven.

I was always tall for my age, and that water was up to my ribs and rising. Daddy went first with Jimbo on one shoulder and the potato sack thrown across the other. Out front porch was high, and we stayed there with Momma until Daddy had time to sit Jimbo high enough on the hill that he would be safe for a while. After he had done that, he came and got us; snatching little Annie right off the tit so Momma could care for Robert, who was crying and throwing a hellacious fit. She picked up Robert to carry him; I did the same for Marybeth and Ben: carrying one on each hip.

The distance from the porch to the back of the house, and then on to the foot of the hill, was maybe a couple hundred feet—not too bad. But when you're trying to hold on to two scared kids and you're walking through cold, deep water…well, two hundred feet seemed like two miles. Ben had his little fingernails dug in me so deep it left bruises. Marybeth hid her face in my neck; I could feel her sobbing. We trudged on; one family, cold and scared out of our wits.

Daddy sat Jimbo propped up against a big beech tree about thirty or forty feet up from the brown rushing creek. In that same tree Daddy had carved with his pocket knife a big heart with "HM + JDM" many years before, on or around their wedding day. I always loved that big beech. Momma did too; when we made it there and collected Jimbo, she took a minute to close her eyes and rested her forehead on it; like the way she used to rest her head on Daddy's chest when she thought nobody was looking. Daddy was preoccupied trying to calm Jimbo, who although was barely audible, was heaving and convulsing to beat the band. Poor little feller probably thought we had left him there alone to die. But once he had calmed down Daddy picked him up again and we started up that mountain.

Everyone knew who to hang on to, and who to pull. Daddy left his footprints long and deep in the mud and dirt, so we all knew exactly where to step. And we were glad of it, because all that rain had washed down the loose dirt and tree tops from the higher elevations. Whereas normally we could have scaled Buncombe straight up, this time we had to zigzag to and fro. Momma led us all in singing her favorite church hymns to keep our minds occupied and to keep us feeling sorry for ourselves. But we were all sad; none of us knew when we'd see our old house again. And I regretted not trying to convince Daddy to carry more stuff; like Momma's guitar, or his reproduction of the Jesse and Frank James tintype he bought at the five-and-dime in Russellville. He loved that old picture.

Halfway up the mountain Marybeth got fussy with me. She said I was pulling too rough and hurting her. I tried telling her that I was being as gentle as I could be; that I was at the mercy of Randy's pulling; and he of Momma's pulling; but she paid me no attention. To keep her from crying I told Robert to switch with her; which they did, so I ended up pulling him instead. But that left the problem of Ben: if Marybeth couldn't handle holding on to me and to Robert, then I knew she couldn't hold on to Ben, the littlest. He was a "wiggler," as Momma used to say. Whereas Robert could be counted on to stay put in one place like a sack of taters, Ben moved and wiggled all the time. So I told everybody to hold on for a minute while I switched with Marybeth, so Randy could pull her. I took my chances and carried Ben in my right arm and pulled Robert with my left. So then we were basically two separate groups zigzagging up the steep, slick mountain. I felt like Sisyphus. I still do.

Now before I get to the part of the story where I talk about what happened to Robert, I'll need to rest. I'm old and I'm tired and even seventy-four years after he went to Heaven telling this tale takes a lot out of me, as you can imagine. Especially the part about when the Rescue Squad and Daddy finally found my little brother— several days after the rain stopped and the water went down—and saw that the turtles and other varmints found him first; his little body with his clothes torn away and the bite marks on the fleshy parts, like his legs and bottom and face. And about the closed-casket funeral inside Doc McInnis' house because our house was still a mess from the flood. And about how Momma didn't allow me to go to the funeral because she blamed me for killing her baby. I'll get to all of that; but you'll have to bear with me—I can't talk about that stuff without bawling. Just know that God didn't give all us mountain folk special feet after all.

But before I talk about all that—and before I have you and everyone else reading your story hating me too—I want to talk about my life after the spring of forty-five. I want you to know I tried to be the best person I could be.

Needless to say Momma and Daddy didn't have a lot to do with me after what happened. That Christmas I didn't get no presents. I had to eat my suppers away from the table, away from the rest of my family. And I prayed every night that the Lord would take me too. And not in my sleep; no, I wanted to hurt. I wanted to be doused in gasoline and set on fire—to prepare myself for Hell, which I knew awaited me.

The following February I turned sixteen and knew it was time to leave. I met a boy and I didn't love him, but he loved me. He was nineteen, so I guess he wasn't a boy, really. He was a bank teller in town; not a looker, exactly—but tall and built and seemed to have a good head on his shoulders. I didn't wait for him to ask for my hand in marriage; I just started talking about it one day and didn't stop until he bought me a little ring and took me to the Justice of the Peace. I didn't go back to the old house for my clothes or nothing. He—Virgil was his name—said he had a little saved so he bought me a few dresses and some shoes and we rented a place a town, so he could walk to work.

By the end of summer, I was pregnant; and by that time Virgil had accepted a loan officer job in Marrowbone. We moved there and bought a little house. I took up sewing and alterations to make a little extra money. We bought a house and two acres just before our twins James and Robert were born in June 1947. While I was recuperating after the long labor, Virgil borrowed his father's beat up old truck and went to Mommy and Daddy's house, asking them to come by and see the babies any time they wanted. Momma slammed the door in his face. Daddy went around back and caught up with Virgil before he started the pickup and asked how I was doing. He told him I was doing fine; and he said that made Daddy smile.

I became the Sunday School teacher for the little kids at Marrowbone Christian Church. I loved that so very much. I missed my family back home in Squalor Hollow, but was hurt that no one came to see me. So I made a promise to myself that I would never hurt a child, no matter what. And I am proud to say I kept that promise until 1997or '98, when my grandson Scott—your father, Scarlet—came home one day wearing a Creed hoodie. It was a kneejerk reaction, one I'm sure no one could fault me for, and I slapped him. Twice. And I felt bad afterwards, but only for a little while. Where I'm from, we respect music.

That Christmas I bought him two Beastie Boys shirts and a Foo Fighters beanie. He apologized for being a pussy. I told him all was forgiven, but to watch his language. He should have used the term "beta."

Well, back to my story.

By the time the twins could use the toilet Virgil had been promoted to bank manager. And with that job came a secretary. A pretty blonde one. I was the last one to find out what was going on, and by then it was too late—he had gotten her pregnant. He agreed to pay the mortgage on our little place until it was paid off, and the court ordered a monthly payment to me and the boys that he agreed was fair. So that was that: no more Virgil…and I didn't mind one bit.

When the boys started school I took a job at the general store and kept sewing an altering clothes for folks. I bought a used car, an old Plymouth, and one Sunday after church I took the boys to see Grandma and Grandpa McLintock. Daddy was happy to see us, and even Momma warmed up to the twins after a while. Daddy told them stories about Frank and Jesse James and the boys hung on his every word. Ben and Marybeth were overjoyed to meet their cousins. Randy was in Korea. He never made it home.

Years passed and the kids grew up and the older folks died. Momma was already an old woman when she got bit by that copperhead. Normally that wouldn't have killed an adult, but by the time Daddy got in from the woods to take her to the hospital, the poison had already worked itself all the way through her body. She suffered a week in Dreckly County General before she passed. Daddy made it to that winter before he just gave up. He took a rope to that big beech tree and then hung hisself from the lowest branch. I wish he coulda stuck around longer to see my boys grow up.

My boys were brilliant students, but that's the only thing they had in common. James graduated at the top of Marrowbone High in sixty-five. Robert was second. Robert went on to enlist in the Marines and James went off to school to study theater. Robert served two tours in Vietnam and met a girl there. They got married and had a boy: Scott. Robert earned a purple heart and returned home a war hero. He's got a big spread in Fayette County now, just down the road from the house Johnny Depp bought for his momma. James, after he graduated, moved to New York and got the AIDS. He moved back home in eighty-six. I took care of him as long as I could, but hospice said he'd be better off in a hospital. He died February 12, 1987 at Good Samaritan in Lexington. That was the second hardest day of my life.

Now before I finish my story, sweet girl, I need to rest. Talking takes a lot out of me. So let Granny rest for a couple hours, then I promise to tell you the rest. I'll tell you about losing my footing, dropping Ben and letting Robert's hand slip out of mine, and having to make the most difficult split-second decision anyone has ever made. I'll tell you everything. I promise.

{Editor's note: Clementine McLintock did not awake from her nap. She passed away peacefully from this Earth December 9, 2018 in her home. At the time of her death she was surrounded by loved ones: her grandson Scott McLintock and his wife Sarah; and their daughter Scarlet. Clemmy, as she liked to be called, was eighty-nine years of age}

Scales

The dream always begins the same.

It's pitch black and I'm walking alone. I don't recognize the
road, but it is paved, double-laned, and I can barely see what
was once freshly-painted white lines and feel the rumble
strips beneath my old black Doc Martens. Around me is a
void; nothing to be found whatsoever. No trees or fields or
buildings to speak of. It is darker than any place I've ever
known, and I am not afraid.

There is no sound. I feel as if I'm breathing, but I
cannot hear it to confirm. Even my heavy footsteps do not

cause enough of a stir in the still, black earth to produce even the faintest complaint. I am just where I want to be: alone with my thoughts. Alone to ponder Proust and recall song lyrics from my youth. Alone and almost happy, to be sure. Unfamiliar feelings these are, though I know with certainty I am dreaming and soon enough life and noise and chaos will consume me yet again. Alone, and knowing what is about to come. Yes, I know what is about to happen, as I have said before: the dream always starts the same. So, in the moment, I will enjoy the solitude and mindfulness ballyhooed famously by Siddhartha and Kerouac and Thoreau. Nothing lay ahead of me, and I am in love with it.

I try to sing but no words escape me. No matter, I tell myself. Enjoy the quiet. I am alone in this Solipsist's wet dream and I am free to conjure and create as I see fit. But for now, I tell myself, just leave it be. Let the stillness be enough. This is the universe before the singularity. I am in the pre-Planck. I am by myself and I am alive. For the moment, your humble author is the alpha and the omega; so, like a child, I spread my arms and spin around and around. For there is no one to see and mock me; furthermore, there is nothing that can trip me up – no pebbles or twigs, flora or fauna. Earth itself, for the moment, is nothing more than a black canvas on which I stand alone as Master.
Spinning, I can feel the wind as I try to mimic the globe's thousand-mile-an-hour whirl on its equatorial axis. Still hearing nothing and seeing nothing, feeling the air upon me is the most exciting and exhilarating sensation I have ever known. No earthly delights nor pleasures of the flesh are its tantamount; however, I begin to feel the inevitable doubt that invariably causes the crash in this sweet little dream-slash-break from reality.

I conclude the spinning nonsense and resume the heel-toe of a grown man. I think of my good friend and fellow Colonel (Colonel only in the sense that Hemingway said every man from Kentucky is a Colonel by birth) Ez Baril; and I find myself wishing I had his innate gift of finding the perfect words for this moment, so as to put pen to paper once I awake. Envy: thy name is *moi*. Envy: my oldest friend. Dark envy of the bleeding-out kind. The kind with the unintended consequence of finding myself alone; such as I am here, in this place where the only thing is absence.

And I start to feel bad.

Now the darkness is becoming heavy, as if a big, black blanket is starting to wrap itself around me. No, I am wrong. Not a blanket, but a python. These are not rumble strips I'm stepping on, but scales. I realize I'm unable to produce a sound for no other reason than I am being slowly suffocated by a serpent that allows in no light and it is just merely toying with me. Watching me as I clumsily dance upon its scales and transfer to it the contents of my human lungs. My racing heart will only entice the thing, I tell myself; so, I pace my breathing, as was taught to me in the Zen Center years before and during a much happier time. It helps, but nothing stops the tightening. It's all in my head, but the constricting causes pain in my chest; my ribs feeling as if they're about to crack and splinter as I continue to walk. Walking now with each step measured, careful and quick. I feel the glowing eyes before I hear the sound. They're burning into my back, just as they have before, but I'm too afraid to break stride; somehow reckoning that the consequences of stopping will be far worse than the consequences of continuing. But in action and inaction, there are always consequences. Life is just a game of balancing the two: action and inaction. There is no right or wrong because literally nothing matters, and not just here in the pre-Planck. The scaly roads I walked--ribs a crackin'--in my wake as well in my sleep mean precisely the same: jack shit.

Realizing and coming to peace with my inevitable and non-negotiable end, I no longer care to soften my stride.

I'll make the bastard work for it. The eyes are closer and they're hot on my skin. They get hotter as I begin to hear the sound. It rolls to me steadily, *mors machina*, this sound comparable to a faraway train or the gallops of the four horsemen inching their way toward me. Eyes aglow, hotter on my back still, and now going completely around me, illuminating the nothingness, if that is possible.

The deathly noise is right behind me and the eyes of the beast begin to jump, to zigzag a little. The bastard is toying with me. The sound, that infernal racket, is now as much a part of my own being as my pulse; and it no longer frightens me. In fact, I welcome what is about to transpire. No more games, no more waiting. The sound is against my back and the eyes are burning right through me as I lift both arms, and extend the middle finger of both hands. I will go down swinging.

The noise is now the idle of a 1978 Ford F-100 pickup truck, now stopped right beside me. The eyes are its headlights, dulled and gray. Behind the wheel: a dark, frail figure, completely black as though it was made of shadows, except for the burning orange-red of a lit cigarette between the black lips. I can smell the grease and sawdust though I am still standing outside the black rustbucket. The passenger window is either rolled down or missing altogether, allowing me to look inside; and that is where I see the heavy thermos. Everything is black, but I know this thermos; I know with certainty it is green and heavy and dented on one side. I know this thermos.

Politely, I wait for the figure to invite me in, or to acknowledge me in any way. Sometimes, in my dream, it does; however, most nights, as in this night, there is no motion. This *being*, my opaque chauffer, my crepuscular companion, only peers straight ahead, past his sharp, pointed nose and under a pitch-black trucker hat, into the void. I can make out the lips slowly suckling at the disgusting cancer stick, causing its hue to deepen and redden and withdraw momentarily toward what I suspect to be a mouthful of tobacco-stained teeth. I'm simultaneously afraid and unafraid. The only harm that can be done to me now is psychological, I deduce, which fills me with confidence; for I can suppress pain of this sort like no other. Gone is the pain of panic and impending doom that nearly crippled me beforehand. I welcome anything and everything that may come.

"3:10 to Yuma?" I jest. Waiting for an answer of any sort would've been foolish, I well knew, so finding the door handle I pull it open and am met with that detestable shrill shriek often associated with rusty doors of aged vehicles. Even in my dreaming state it is enough of a hideous cacophony to take me aback momentarily; nonetheless, finding my footing, I move aside the old thermos and plop my fat ass in the seat. The truck lurches forward before both cheeks are down, and two men with nothing to offer the twenty-first century were in motion, with no destination and no timetable for arrival.

He said nothing. The minutes felt like hours. Every time I had this dream he never spoke. Sometimes I chose to ignore the fact that it was an exercise in futility and attempted to engage the driver – asking him how he was doing, how long he had been behind the wheel, etc. Sometimes I would tell jokes, thinking levity would stir him out of his inner doldrums. Nothing worked. So some nights I was content just sitting in the truck as it (presumably) advanced forward.

In my dream on this night, I was feeling rather loquacious. I thanked him for picking me up, saying I wasn't sure how long I could have continued, nor where I was headed. I asked his destination? He did not answer, choosing instead to smoke his damned cigarette and stare straight ahead.

We had done this dance many times before.

A man considered prolix, such as myself, would not allow silence to be a setback; especially when such a man had something to prove. Undaunted, I took a stab at humor: asking the driver if he had heard the one about the twelve-inch pianist. He gave no hint if he even heard me.

The cigarette smelled more of sulfuric hellfire than tobacco. It permeated my entire face, principally my nostrils and behind my eyeballs. The stench was pure evil, less Camel and more bowels of the Darvaza crater, deep in the Karakum desert. The wretched thing, it burned bright red, redder than anything I had beheld before. It gave no light to the driver's face, if indeed it was a face. I was not afraid until the laws of physics were bent, for nothing would illuminate this man.

"I've kept my promise, Pop." I continued, slowly and with each syllable clear. "I meant every word. Mom and Sis are okay."

Nothing. Not even a sigh.

"Mom's in a good home. She's confused a lot--strokes'll do that to ya. And Sis: the facility she goes to every day helps people like her. It's called Daybreak Adult Care. They even pick her up in the morning and bring her home in the afternoon."

The truck continued forward, I decided a cessation of my pathetic rambling was best. Again, the minutes felt like hours. The headlights of the shitrustbucket barely broke the pitch black night. The thermos pitched between us, my father and I, and finally I placed my hand on it, so as to keep it from bumping our legs.

"I'm a dad now, too. Yep, my little girl is three now, and she's so smart. You'd love her." I suppose I said that last part to remind the driver that, in fact, he was dead. He had died from lung cancer in 2006, shortly after my twenty-eighth birthday. In my last conversation with him, just two days before his death, I had promised him that I would take care of my mother and sister. Mom was getting older, and Sis was stricken with cerebral palsy at birth. I lived in a city two hundred miles away at the time, and in order to fulfill my promise I knew I'd have to move back home to the town of Mooresville, deep down in the Commonwealth, though I detested living there as a child and as a teenager. Leaving for college was the best thing I ever did for myself.

I decided against laying a guilt-trip on the old man, reminding him that my life in Ohio was good and I gave it up to adhere to my word. I chose not to say it because he knew it. I assume he knew everything. I also assume he knew why he was angry with me, though, for the life of me, I did not know. For years the question plagued my days and haunted my nights: why did he hate me? Several times during our journey in my dreams I asked him. He never answered. Not once. His lack of answers frequently angered me, but always saddened me. I begged for a clue, just one. Nothing.

On this night, in this dream, I chose not to continue my pathetic pandering for his attention. I instead decided to do what I do better than anyone else: I busted his balls. "So whatcha doing these days? Are you *up*, or are you *down*? Do you finger-blast Annie Oakley in a barn made of clouds, or do you help ol' Thomas Ketchum look for his head in the brimstone? Or, are you in-between: spending your time driving this piece of shit looking for hitchhikers and then boring the shit out of them?

"Do you spend eternity thinking of new ways to fuck with me? To make me your Sisyphus, pushing the rock of your angst bullshit uphill for the rest of my days? Asshole. Should I resign myself to *amor fati*? Say something, you son of a bitch!"

It was pointless for me to become angry. It would do no good. It was usually around this point in the dream that I would awaken, but not on this night. We continued driving with not a word muttered for quite some time. I do not know if I cried or if I just sat in anger; but what is certain is that I felt more alone than I did when I was walking the scaly road all to myself.

Four billion years of evolution, and we have failed. If today's man is the best we can do given that amount of time, then we do not deserve to live on a planet with water, in the goldilocks zone just the right distance from the sun allowing us to flourish. No better example of this can be found than with these two men, father and son. Growing up, he was one of a very few people than saw my three-dimensional self. He accepted, early-on, that I was a loser. He accepted this, though, because he knew I was not pretentious. I did not pretend to be anything more than a loser, and he respected that. In fact, we bonded over it. Dad knew what I lacked in intelligence and gumption I made up for in heart. That is why he placed the care of my sister in my hands, not with my older brothers. We looked alike, Dad and I, and we got along pretty well most of my life. That is, until he got sick, then, for some reason none of us knew, his attitude toward me changed. That was twelve years ago now. Twelve bitter years. Twelve confusing years.

There were so many things I wanted to say in this dream, mostly negative, though I also longed to tell him about my life now. To tell him that I followed his footsteps and have landed in the lumber business, learning to grade and price. To show him photographs of my daughter and tell him that she has his smile and my mean streak. But I couldn't. Not anymore.

"I'm giving you one chance, old man. One chance to talk to me, about anything you want. One chance to get anything off your chest. But if you don't, if you choose to be a pussy, then I'm letting this shit go. And I mean for good."

I think he grinned, but I woke up.

Enfant Terrible

He followed the instructions perfectly, as he did every Friday. Parked roughly the length of a football field away from his daughter's school, Rhys sat in his Corolla and listened to Korn's *Follow the Leader*, the recently released twentieth anniversary edition, and wondered where the time went. He looked at the

Vincero watch on his heavily tattooed arm (the watch was a birthday gift from his little girl) and saw it was three o' clock. Any minute now. He threw his copy of John Fante's masterpiece *Ask the Dust* from the passenger seat to the back seat.

He continued to listen to the music, and the music carried him back in time. Back to a previous life altogether it seemed. Back to when all that mattered was music and ink and books; all shared with friends that would never go away. Friends that would never lose touch or move across the country or die.

Rhys reminisced about following Korn the summer of 2000 during Metallica's *Summer Sanitarium* tour. *Kids today: they just don't know,* he thought to himself. And then he wondered how the hell he avoided being killed in one of the dozens of mosh pits that sweltering season. Perhaps it was for this moment: waiting outside a school to pick up his daughter that was ashamed to be seen with him; hence having to park on the other side of town, basically. Life is funny that way.

He looked again at his watch. Not because he was unsure of the time, but because of the good memory it brought back. His birthday the previous year; back when things seemed a bit less complicated and hectic. Back when little Oona would squeeze his neck in public. The blue face and chocolate brown leather wristband made him happy. It was the accessory he built his daily wardrobe around. He had wanted a Vincero for some time, but splurging for a gift for himself was out of the question. Things change when you're a family man. And yes, to Rhys, spending a couple hundred bucks on himself was an unnecessary extravagance. Especially since dropping nearly a grand on dance classes for his daughter.

He glanced up to see her exiting the school. She was beautiful, the spitting image of her mom. Oona held her head high, smiling and nodding goodbye to her friends on her way to meet her ride. She was tall and all legs; frightfully thin despite inheriting her dad's healthy appetite. Her aqua blue backpack seemed too wide for her frail shoulders. And once she saw her old man waiting down the street in his old man car, she hastened her pace, lowered her chin, and folded her skinny arms across her chest in obvious embarrassment. It was as if she was trying to disappear into herself. He realized the music was louder than she liked, so he lowered the volume as she reached for the door handle.

"Good afternoon, offspring! How was school?"

"Dad," she replied, "don't be such a dork." She said this having yet to look him in the eye. She sat as low in the passenger seat as possible and then buckled her safety belt before realizing she might have come off a bit rude. "It was fine, Dad. Just like every other day."

Just like always, Rhys pulled at her safety belt as an added measure before merging with the other cars picking up their unappreciative little tax shelters. He himself only wore a safety belt when Oona was in the car with him—setting a good example, as a father should.

"Dad, not so close," Oona said as she slid further into her seat, as if the bottom of it were a black hole she was being sucked into. "That's Tessa in front of us."

"In the Tesla? Tessa's in the Tesla?" Rhys laughed. He thought it was funny; but only he thought so. (Dad jokes often miss their mark.) He stayed back to allow space between himself and the new pearl white Model X immediately ahead of him at Oona's behest.

"Jesus, Dad...you make that joke every time."

"Well, I'm sorry, honey; but it's funny. And please...the language. We've talked about the language, remember?"

"How could I forget?"

"I know I've said it a lot, but it's for your own good. And mine. You know every time you say 'Jesus' or 'goddamn' your grandparents complain to your mother. And your mother, my beloved wife, yells at me because..."

"Because you come from white trash?"

"Precisely."

"Okay. I'll do better."

"Thank you, sweetheart."

They continued on in silence for some time. Oona, to her credit, defied her natural instinct to remove her phone from her back pocket and stare at its screen like a braindead simpleton. She did this as a show of respect for her father; and he took note of it. He knew that she made those little sacrifices for him—the seemingly innocuous ones that commonly go unnoticed. Though he did not want to mention it specifically, he did want to reward her somehow.

"So, sweetheart, I was thinking…let's go to a Reds game this weekend. You know, like we used to."

She looked at him inquisitively. "The Reds? Don't they suck this year?"

"Oh, very much so. But that is no different than every other year. Besides, it's September. And we both know those dipshits won't be playing in October."

This made Oona laugh a little, though she would never admit it. Parents stop being funny at certain but undefinable age. He could tell she was scouring the deepest recesses of her brain for any excuse to say no and politely decline the invitation, so he decided to spare her the discomfort.

"Oh, that's right; I forgot. Your mother is taking you to that Lily Pulitzer store this weekend."

She was visibly relieved. And he was visibly dispirited.

"Yeah, sorry Dad. Maybe next season. Though, for the record, Lily clothes look like someone ate a bunch of paint and puked it back up."

"Yep. I never was a fan." And that was true. For years his wife spent an ungodly amount of money on dresses and tops and even comforters that he could only describe as "clown bukkake."

"Lily Pulitzer is just Ed Hardy for stuck-up white women," said Oona. And Rhys wondered if anyone had ever loved anything more than he loved is daughter at that moment.

"So, honey, would it be weird if I brought in my laptop during your dance class today? I don't want to be a distraction, but I need to catch up on some stuff for work. Would that be okay?"

Oona's eyes widened and her mouth went agape. "You mean," she said with face contorted in abject horror, "you're coming inside?"

Rhys felt as if he was just punched in the gut. It took the wind right out of him.

"Well, yeah…I mean, it crossed my mind. Doesn't your mother come in?"

Oona stared at him unflinchingly. It was as if she too had been punched in the gut.

It was at this point that all his fears had surfaced. Rhys did the math in his head. He was fifty years old, heavily tattooed, a little on the chunky side, and worked as a book-balancer for a sawmill. Oona was twelve, absolutely brilliant and gorgeous; with friends aplenty. And these friends of hers had parents that were younger and more prominent; better looking and thinner.

He was officially and irrevocably an embarrassment.

"It's okay, sweetie. I'll just stay in the car. The Wi-Fi should be plenty strong out there anyway."

Oona smiled with relief. "Thanks, Dad."

The theater that played host to her practice and recitals was across town, and traffic was crawling at three-fifteen on a Friday afternoon. Oona confirmed that she was wearing her dance attire under her clothes, in case they were so pressed for time that she needed to practically tuck-and-roll out of the moving car to be punctual. Rhys noticed his daughter's black fingernail polish and smiled proudly. A chip off the old punk block, though she would never admit to being anything like her old man. He was fairly certain she was the only one on the dance team that had black nails, and this made him so proud. Tessa, for example, was the prototypical girly-girl that he, and the world, rightfully despised. Her nails were always freshly pink or blue; her hair was always fashioned to mimic the style of the latest pop-tart atop the Billboard chart; her clothes consistently clown bukkake.

Bitch chic, he called it. Just as he had in the eighties, the nineties, etc.

"Is everyone being nice to you?"

"What do you mean?" she asked without looking at him.

"Well," he began, "I remember a while back you had some issues with some of the girls. Like, I don't know...Tessa, for example."

He could tell she did not want to talk about it; or even acknowledge it any way.

"Oh, that...um, yeah. Everything is fine. I get along fine with everyone." He knew she was lying because as she said this, for the first time she removed her phone from her back pocket and began scrolling through her newsfeed. His internal struggle to press the matter nearly surfaced; but he had learned that that was no way to get reach his daughter—or any female, for that matter. Besides, if the situation called for it, he knew his little girl was a fighter. Just like her old man. And he pitied the girl that might have to find that out the hard way.

"Okay. Just checking. Not trying to pry, just curious." They were only minutes away from their destination, which was good and bad. She wasn't going to be late, but he did not get to spend enough time with his daughter, and he hated that. The commute in heavy traffic went by too quickly for his liking. In the blink of an eye she, his absolutely perfect daughter, went from a baby to a toddler to a preteen. Blink again and she'll be at her prom, then college, then somewhere bigger and better and far, far away. And he would just get older and fatter and die all alone.

"Oh! she said, "I almost forgot...I need some money," Oona said still staring at her phone. "Ted's birthday is this weekend; we're pooling money today to get him a gift card."

"Ted? Tesla Ted? Rhys asked. "Doesn't he have enough money?" And in that moment Rhys realized he had finally turned into *his* father.

"Fine. Forget I said anything."

Rhys hated this game. "Okay," he said. How much does Tesla Ted need?"

"I don't know. Forty. Fifty, maybe."

Rhys gripped the steering wheel until his knuckles turned pure white. His teeth clenched. However, he ignored his natural instinct to teach his daughter about the value of money, and with teeth welded shut, took his wallet from his back pocket. He then handed it to his daughter. "Here," he said. "Just take out what you think is right."

Oona took the wallet from her dad and removed two twenty dollar bills so deftly that it actually worried him.

"Thanks, Dad," she said while handing the wallet back.

"Sure. Anything for Tesla Ted. How old is he turning, by the way?"

"Thirty-nine, I think Tessa said. We're getting him a Brooks Brothers gift card. It's his favorite store."

Rhys turned up the volume on the radio to muffle the screams in his head.

"Well," he began, "good for him."

"Tessa said his store is doing really good."

"*Well*, honey...his store is doing *well*."

"Yeah. Sorry. Well. Anywho, did you ever think of doing something like that? Opening a store or shop or something?" she asked. "Mom said your retirement plan was to open a bookstore. And Lord knows you have enough books for it." She peered over her left shoulder to see the backseat of the Corolla looked like a tornado had ripped through a college English Lit course. Strewn about were Bukowski, Kerouac, Miller, Mailer, Nin...her old man was literally never without a novel at arm's length.

"Well, funny enough you ask...because just today I was thinking about opening a store," he said straight-faced.

"Really?" she asked, turning her body to face him.

"Yep. I had a brilliant idea for the perfect store" and as he said this, his hand secretly and swiftly hit the child window safety lock button. His hand moved so sneakily that Oona didn't even notice.

"Well?"

"Well what?" he asked, pretending to not understand the question.

"What kind of store, ya big dummy?"

Oh…that. Well, I was thinking of opening a fart store." As he said this, he rolled his weight, strategically lifting one ample ass cheek off his seat.

"A *what* store?" she asked, obviously confused. As soon as she asked this, she realized she knew that answer. And her old man ripped the biggest fart she had ever heard in her whole life. His second-biggest of the day.

"Oh my God!" she exclaimed while trying to roll down her window to no avail. "What the hell's the matter with you?" The volume of her yells were equaled by the volume of his laughter. The more she coughed and covered her nose from the rancid stench the more happy-tears rolled down his cheek. When he determined she had had enough, he rolled down her window halfway.

"I'm sorry, baby. I just had to" he said, still laughing. He looked over to see that Oona, though still with her nose and mouth covered by her shirt, was laughing too. But then she noticed he was watching her; and, upon realizing this, reverted back to her normal sullen visage.

"Sometimes I think Grandma and Grandpa are right," he heard her mumble.

She could be brutal—tiny, but brutal. Rhys knew what she meant.

After an extended silence, he feigned the biggest smile he was capable of just as they pulled up to the theater. Rhys used his right hand to rub the watch on his left wrist before hitting the release button on Oona's safety belt. It was 3:26.

"I'll go to the coffee shop across the street. Just text when you're ready to leave. I'll make sure not to leave until all the other girls have been picked up." His face then produced a pitiful grin as he told Oona to break a leg.

"Thanks, Dad. I'll text you." She said this while jumping out of the car and hurriedly walked along the cobblestone path leading to the theater's front doors.

His car was parked in a handicap spot, but only briefly, as to let his daughter have the shortest walk possible to her practice. Even after she disappeared inside, Rhys sat in his car in quiet contemplation. He would not have traded being a father for anything—all the riches in this world and the promise of heaven in the one after; but, he was not prepared for times like this. The thought that he would one day be Quasimodo to the thing he loved most never occurred to him. Fifty is too old to be sad. Just as he thought this, there was a knock on his passenger window. It was Oona.

"Hi, honey…did you forget something?' he asked after rolling down her window.

"No, Dad, I just wanted to say…well, it's not true..."

He looked at his daughter inquisitively.

"…you are not white trash," she continued. Oona lovingly leaned in through the window as far as she could, just so Rhys could fully understand her.

Though her face was one of seriousness, he could not help but to smile. "Well, thank you, offspring…but that just tells me you're a lousy judge of character." He winked.

Oona smiled, then laughed. It was not a little laugh; it was a big one—like the laughs she used to emit when he would blow on her belly to make fart noises. Back when Oona not just loved her old man, but *liked* him too. She looked at him the way she once did, as she did on the day when she presented him with the fancy watch. Then she returned herself to standing position, pulling her long torso outside the vehicle. Then looking at her father, said "Jesus, Dad, don't be such a dork."

She winked back.

The Sawmill

Even as the day's first rays began to irradiate the world around him, Cal Tidwell, standing safely inside his humble law office behind a locked door, eyed with contempt his dreary surroundings at the corner of Main and Lincoln. Just five years out of law school and with a track record of only cases settled or dismissed, he was dreadfully unready for the litigation that would either make or break his young career. His third cup of morning coffee sat untouched on a Cincinnati Reds coaster, on an oak table in his unostentatious office that was once a nail parlor. It was a Sunday morning and early enough that even the meth heads were still slumbering. He began to reach for his joe when the unmistakable sound of a new Japanese sport bike pulled up outside his lobby window. Cal rolled down the sleeves of his pale blue Brooks Brothers shirt and adjusted his tie, making the knot just the perfect amount of off-centeredness, according to the online tutorial from *The Gentleman's Gazette*, that businessmen and sartorial experts find ideal.

Carmelo Avalos, Cal noted, looked not unlike the countless other migrant workers that had come to Mooresville to find work in a sawmill or at a construction site. His receptionist, thankfully bi-lingual and quite adept at capturing even the most minute of details in shorthand, jotted Carmelo was twenty-seven years old and unmarried. He had been with his employer for two years prior to the accident. According to Julie's meticulous notes, he had received a settlement of forty-one thousand dollars from Mooresville Lumber and Pallet. That figure being roughly two years' salary for the young lumber stacker. Knowing this, Cal assumed the shiny blue Yamaha R1 parked in a handicapped spot outside his office was paid in full. He watched as Carmelo removed his helmet and dismounted, ever so gingerly, the young attorney's dream bike. Cal unlocked the front door then stepped away four or five paces, so as not to appear too eager.

The chime announced Carmelo's entrance; and, for the first time, the law office of T. Calum Tidwell hosted the young man whose name had become a running joke throughout the county. He was wearing camo cargo shorts, high black Doc Marten boots, and a Houston Astros Jose Altuve jersey with a layer of dead bugs discoloring what was, before he sat on his bike that morning, sparkling white. Carmelo smiled genially, walked, grimacing with each measured step, and extended his hand to the proprietor. Cal accepted with trepidation.

"Before we get started, you need to know that I don't speak a lick of *espanol*. I can't afford no translator, and I only speak in English, *comprende*?"

"Yes, I understand," replied the short, slight migrant, who noticeably cringed at the attorney's double-negative.

"Good. Now listen, you were told to park around back. You were told, explicitly, to park in the lot behind my office; not in front of it. If I'm going to take your case, you must listen and understand everything I say, got it?"

"Yes. I apologize. I will move my motorcycle now."

"Too late. Too damn late. Even on a Sunday enough people saw you, and heard you, on that damn thing, pulling into my lot and parking right next to me. Take a seat. Coffee?"

"No, thank you. It makes me nervous, and I am already much nervous."

For a moment, Cal felt badly for being so uncouth with the young man. Internally, he blamed his acerbity on the hour, seeing as how he was not a morning person. Notwithstanding, he himself asked Julie to set up their initial convocation at seven on a Sunday morning. Fewer people about and fewer distractions. And, if being completely honest with himself, fewer town gossips speculating what a local, unmarried attorney was doing alone on a Sunday morning with the likes of Carmelo Avalos behind closed doors.

Accepting his host's invitation to do so, Carmelo took a seat in a second-hand black leather chair in the cramped and dim office that still faintly smelled of acrylic. Cal took the big chair on the powerful side of the table, beneath the cheap gold plastic frame encasing his JD from Chase Law that he received five years prior. Oddly enough, Carmelo observed, his undergraduate degree from Centre College in Danville was much more prominently displayed, and in a beautiful gray driftwood frame.

Before either party said a word, Cal sized-up the timid young man that sought him out for help. Calum was not what one would call a large man; but, he was close to a foot taller than Carmelo and perhaps eighty or ninety pounds heavier. This instinctively caused him to sit even straighter in his nice, tall chair. He wondered how someone so slight could stack lumber for two years, working for a company that was notorious for taking shortcuts when it came to safety and general working conditions. Cal was familiar with Mooresville L&P, having worked there as a lumber stacker the summer between high school and college. Well, not the whole summer. He had intended to work there two months to make money for school; however, he barely lasted two weeks. The job was just too much for him. Too many splinters; too many blackened fingernails; too many early mornings.

Carmelo, Cal recognized, was not built like the other migrant workers in town: he was sinewy with muscle, and not blocky like the rest. His features were delicate, not leathery and hewn. Then he remembered the reason for their meeting.

"So I heard about the accident. How are you doing? Physically, I mean; we'll get to psychologically later." His olfactory perceptions, already heightened more than most, detected his guest was wearing perfume heavy with jasmine. It was pleasant to him, and he was delighted it would at least temporarily mask the smell of acrylic and ass on second-hand leather.

"Not good. But, a little better day by day. The bark, and the chain, it took my balls. Took my penis. Cut my legs real bad. I bled real bad. Almost died." Carmelo said this as if rehearsed; or, if not rehearsed, then told and retold many times.

"I know, and I'm sorry. But before we get into the details, how many lawyers did you go to before calling my office? I know it was quite a few, because the word has spread about what you're looking to do, and with the additional money you want."

"I don't know. Five, six maybe. But it's not more money I want, not really. I want the surgery. I want what the sawmill already started."

"Right. But, as you recall, you settled already. You got like forty grand for your injuries."

"Should have been more," replied Carmelo. "Should have been lots more. They humiliated me. Made me take two drug tests that day, even though I pass the first one fine." Tears began welling in his eyes; eyes as big as Sacagawea dollars and brown as a chestnut.

"Well, I'm not going to argue that. Because you're right: if you would have held out any good lawyer could have gotten you several times that amount. Nevertheless, you took the payoff. So why did you do it? Why just forty grand?" Sucking air through his front teeth, Cal immediately recoiled and regretted the words he absent-mindedly chose. *Goddamn Podunk Matlock move*, he chided himself silently.

"*Just* forty grand? What you mean *just*? To you, forty-one thousand is not much. I know this. But to me, to my people, that is a lot. And I do not mean my people as in Mexican-Americans; I mean my people as in people who work all day. They sweat all day. Not in office all day. They get fifteen minutes for lunch. Lunches they eat sitting on the same conveyor belt they stand beside all day. What you mean *just*?" After saying this, Carmelo sat taller and straighter than he ever had in his life. His head was high and his eyes ablaze; his lips did not tremble.

"I'm sorry. I misspoke. It's early, so forgive me. Tell me, then, why did you take the money so quickly?" Backpedaling in this manner was unfamiliar to Cal, but to his surprise he did so suitably and proficiently.

Carmelo slumped slightly in his chair. His legs were so short that his feet, even in boots, practically dangled above the aged, dirty tan carpet beneath them. Cal noted that he barely looked fifteen years old, with those bright brown eyes, caramel skin free of lines, and black hair pulled back into a ponytail.

"Before I answer," Carmelo said, "you answer: how did you know I see other lawyers first? Lawyers not supposed to talk about people that see them, right? People that talk to them, right? *Privilege*, or something, right?"

Cal smirked. *How naïve*, he thought. *Welcome to America, ese.*

"Yes. You are right. But, let's not forget, this is a small town. And nothing is secret in Mooresville. Nothing is sacred in places like this. Especially regarding a situation such as yours. So you better learn this and learn it quickly."

Carmelo was getting a crash course in American Civics, southern style. He sneered at the obvious condescension in Cal's tone. He daydreamed briefly about dragging his host by his purple silk tie into the street and stomping the life out of him.

"Fine. So if you know I see other lawyers before, why you say you see me? If they no take this case, this very good case, then why you say okay come see me?"

The game had now, momentarily, shifted. Cal wanted this case, a freebie though it may be; however, had to appear as if he'd be doing Carmelo, and the entire Mooresville Mexican-American community, a big favor. He had to be Jesus-on-the-cross to them. And that is just how he pictured himself.

"We'll talk about me later. Your questions will be answered, but not until I hear everything from you. So tell me. Tell me what you want. What would make you happy?" Carmelo's spine snapped straight in his chair. It was his turn to say, as eloquently as possible, what he truly wanted from his former employer. Everything he felt entitled to and nothing more. He had practiced his forthcoming spiel many times to himself, and a few times to the other loose-lipped lawyers in Mooresville.

"As you know, the de-barker at the mill, it took my balls. The chain bind and snap as I was walking back to my station, and it hit me in the pants. Just walking; not doing or touching anything. My balls and penis shredded. They practically gone. And my legs will never be the same. My line boss say he never seen so much blood. And my stomach has scars. Bad scars –"

"-and for your injuries you received a generous payment. So what the hell do you want now?"

"Now I want you shut the hell up and listen to me!"

Cal was taken aback by the sudden outburst. He recalled his ex-fiancé saying he can come off as supercilious and mean sometimes. She was right; and she was certainly not the first person to tell him as much. Then he thought that supercilious was the nicest thing he had been called by anyone who had known him for some time. In fact, "asshole" was the standard.

"I apologize. I won't interrupt you again," he lied quite convincingly.

"I want sex change. Complete what the sawmill started. I want to be female. Completely female. And the treatments afterwards. All of it. Therapy too, if I need it. I look online, and it says years of therapy, maybe."

Finally, Cal thought, we had gotten to the crux of the matter. His lawyer buddies in town had been talking about this for a couple weeks. About how Carmelo, the little brown homo, wanted to be a girl. They even talked about what a pretty girl he'd make. Five-foot-two, dark auriferous skin, slender build. Hearing this, Cal began to wonder who the *real* homos in town were.

"And you want Mooresville L&P to foot the bill, right? That'll be a tall order, you understand? You already accepted cash from them. Not a lot of cash, but twice the amount your replacement will make in a year. They'll consider the matter closed. Frankly, I can see their point."

"Then why? Why see me? Why tell your lady to tell me okay come see me Sunday? Why waste our time if you just want to laugh at me too? I bet a big lawyer in a big city would love this case."

Cal knew that Carmelo was right. Sure, a city lawyer would love this case. Potentially even the state chapter of the ACLU would take it. Without showing too much on his face, he studied the figures. The zeros and commas kept coming. He could go after not just the sawmill, but the manufacturer of the sawmill's faulty equipment too. If OSHA had visited the sawmill recently, they failed to notice what would become a life-changing mechanical malfunction. Cal could go after them, too. And if it had been a while since they visited the mill, they could have a vested interest in this case as well. A potential partner; one with deep pockets. Yes, he wanted this case. He wanted it badly. This little homo before him was a goldmine, a little brown goldmine; but, he just could not let him know that. Not yet, at least. If he did, Carmelo might indeed hop his little crippled ass back on his bike and ride into the law offices of the next F. Lee Bailey, whomever he or she may be.

Besides monetarily, Carmelo being under his protection would have added benefits for the tiny law office as well. You see, Calum Tidwell was nothing if not ambitious. Lawyering was just a way to catapult himself to where he belonged: the world of politics. The demographics of Mooresville were changing and changing rapidly. They were turning a deeper hue; not so lily white any longer. Mexican-American families were moving in while Caucasian families were moving out, or dying out altogether. The evidence was all around, as any trip to the local grocery store or restaurant or church would attest. And if Cal Tidwell could get six figures for a client that, regardless of color, was entitled to a big payday, then that is what would have to happen. White people were going to the polls less and less with every election. If he could position himself as a voice for the growing Mexican-American populace, then it would be the perfect opportunity to get himself elected. He would be lauded as a hero on the local news. Hell, maybe even the national news. After the obviously (in his mind) favorable and sizeable verdict or settlement, he could ride the wave to the state House and finally have a Frankfort address. No more driving past trailer parks on the way to work, and seeing buildings that once employed hundreds now decaying like the dead old men that built them.

Shit, he thought. *Should I learn Spanish?*

"So how long have you wanted to be a female? Just since the accident? Since childhood? I ask these tough questions because people much meaner than myself will be asking them, you see. Because if it's been in your head since you were a *niño*, the defense will convince a decrepit old small town judge and jury you're just a little queer looking for taxpayers to take care of you. Do you have a partner? A boyfriend? What does he think about this?"

"No. No partner," was Carmelo's reply. "And I'm no looking for a handout. After surgery, after hormones, I get a job. An office job. Maybe even back at the mill. They have offices with ladies that do paperwork and invoices and stuff. I have always worked and I will always work. Tomorrow is Monday, no? Mondays I was always first one at sawmill. Five in the morning, one hour before clock-in, I be there waiting. I work hard, anyone will tell you--"

--"Wrong," interjected the cocksure young barrister. "No one will tell me that. I know it's true, I do; but, these people literally hate you now. You understand? When you were just a lumber stacker and still in the closet, sure, they would have said you work hard. But this is Kentucky. And you're gay. A Mexican gay –"

--"Mexican-American, assface."

"Fine. Mexican-American. But back to my point: you have told too many people what you want. The surgery; the hormones; the therapy. So how long have you wanted to be a girl?" Cal himself did not know why he kept hammering away at this, with this particular query, but he was convinced it was important enough to warrant an answer.

"Long time. Many years." Carmelo did not know if his answer would work in his favor, or against it. But he told the truth. His quivering lip and reddening eyes made this evident to the attorney.

Things had gotten too heated between the two. Cal reminded himself that at any moment Carmelo could up and leave. He could not allow this to happen. It was time to show his face cards.

"When you talked to the other lawyers in town, how long did they see you? How long before they said 'no' to taking your case? Five minutes? Ten?"

"Few minutes. That is all. That is all the time they would give me. But I have a good case here. A strong case. But they all say the same thing: 'I cannot take you on, cannot take you on, cannot take you on.' Over and over and over. But I am not asking for a dollar more than the cost of surgery and treatments. Therapy, maybe. But I no want more cash."

"Well I do," shot back the attorney. "If I take this on; rather, if I take *you* on, I am going after a big payday. For the both of us. Carmelo, you do not see the big picture. If you listen to me and do everything as I say, we can be rich. And famous, too. You will be a hero, to Mexican-Americans, the workers at the sawmill, and even the transgendered. This case will make headlines, I tell you! The whole state and even the country will take notice. I will show Mooresville Lumber and Pallet put you in unsafe working conditions, were slow to get you the help you needed, and quickly paid you hush money to sweep it all under the rug. The ant in the afterbirth: they were happy to get rid of you because you're a queer. And a Mexican. That they were heartless in their treatment of a good worker following a mishap that he himself was not the cause of. If we play these cards right, we can make hundreds of thousands; and, most importantly, get the hell out of this town and away from these people."

Carmelo sat quietly, staring dead ahead, his jaw slack. Leaving Mooresville never entered his mind. That is when he knew this case, if taken by Cal, would not be about him, nor the mill and its lax safety standards. There was silence between the two, an awkward silence that dragged on. Carmelo looked fixedly forward, unblinking, as if the promise of America that he subscribed to his entire life and taught to him by his parents, now both deceased, was outed as nothing more than a sham. A two hundred year Ponzi scheme. And men like T. Calum Tidwell were the embodiment of the man behind the curtain.

Carmelo no longer had desire to speak. He turned his head slowly from left to right, taking in the entire scene. He gazed at the pictures on the walls; there were not many, but they hung in such a way as to actually deter guests from perusing them. Like the simple eight-by-ten over the right shoulder of his host. It appeared to be Cal smiling and shaking hands with a man-sized turtle in a black suit. He squinted and leaned in slightly, just enough to recognize the turtle as Mitch McConnell. Carmelo only knew his name because the other lawyers in town had very similar photos on their walls. On the right wall, hanging crooked on the brown paneling, was another eight-by-ten; this one of Cal in cap and gown and flanked by older people, presumably his parents. The male looked uncomfortable and out of place in his dress pants, short sleeve white button down shirt and dark tie. The female, plump and dark-headed, wearing a floral dress, feigned a smile. There were no pictures on the desk.

Cal thought Carmelo was staring at him; no, not at him, but through him. The silence lingered, and it vexed him greatly. His face reddened and his forehead began to sweat, his fight-or-flight engaging and throttling his brain stem. It occurred to Cal for the first time that he truly did not *know* the man in front of him. He had a preconceived notion, and he had Julie's notes, but these did not gauge a man's proneness to violence. And, he must not forget, this was Sunday morning and no one was around. He could sense Carmelo's growing anger, and he contemplated the cost of a metal detector on the front door. For all his bravado, Cal knew he could not hold his own in a fight, even against someone much smaller than he. And what if Carmelo had a blade? *A lot of 'em do*, he thought. He was afraid; and the irony was not lost on him. Because if this meeting came to blows, Cal knew he was the one truly lacking balls.

"I like this town. I like these people," Carmelo finally said, breaking the reticence. And with that, he thanked T. Calum Tidwell for his time. He stood slowly, in obvious pain, and took a step toward the door.

"Stop. Please, sit down, Mr. Avalos." His words failed to resonate, as Carmelo continued his progression. Cal stood quickly, and awkwardly bumped his knee on his desk in attempt to catch Carmelo before he left to take his case to another lawyer. "Please, I can help you. Everything you want, I think I can get it. But you need to sit down."

"Thank you for your time. But I go now," Carmelo said indignantly, with a steely, stoic face belying his hurt. Cal placed his hand on Carmelo's shoulder, towering above him, but not using enough force to adequately slow his pace.

"Come on, just five more minutes. That's all I ask." Cal was sweating, his pulse racing; he had the demeanor of a man at the craps table and milliseconds away from going flat broke.

"No. Goodbye."

Cal placed himself squarely in front of Carmelo, just two paces from the door. He said nothing; neither of them did. Cal looked down at Carmelo; Carmelo stared straight ahead, his eyes burning a hole in his host's hundred-dollar shirt. Traffic was beginning to move about on both Main and Lincoln. Two dogs barked as their respective owners passed on the sidewalk. And T. Calum Tidwell grabbed the cheeks of Carmelo Avalos and kissed him deeply.

The kiss could have lasted a second, or a minute. Neither man was sure. As they pulled apart, and the sounds of the town slowly returned to their ears and the overpowering smell of acrylic to their nostrils, they did not speak. Indeed, no words were exchanged, as if both were in shock because of what just transpired.

Carmelo extended his left arm, as if to embrace Cal but instead grabbed for the bar that ran along the front door.

"Wait."

That was all Cal could manage to say. No other words would come.

Carmelo sidestepped him, and pushing the door open said, "Sorry, but I will not take you on."

Second Opinion

I suppose I should have gone straight to work following my appointment, but my house was on the way and I thought my wife should hear the bad news first.

The little bookstore she liked was also on the way, so I stopped in to get her the newest offering from Reese Witherspoon that she had been wanting. I cannot imagine that the book had any sliver of wisdom worth imparting; but this was not for me, I reminded myself as I handed my debit card to the oblivious child working (for lack of a better term) at the sales counter. Joe Hill's latest novel was calling to me from its prominent display immediately beside the register, but following my doctor visit I knew being foolhardy and cavalier with money would be unwise. She, the clerk, was about twenty; barely a hundred pounds, no makeup except mascara that must have been stuck in her eyelashes for ten days. She smelled of absolutely nothing.

"You okay?" asked the typically inconversant and dispassionate girl as she placed the receipt between two random pages of the book that she handed to me without bagging. "You don't look good."

I smiled and exited the bookstore, nodding farewell to the young lady and to Joe Hill. For good measure, I crop-dusted my way through the myriad of slackjaws ogling Kellyanne Conway as she lied from the small television located on the wall above the periodicals. It was a six-egg breakfast, so I am sure they were not pleased.

The short drive to home seemed exceptionally long, but Korn Radio on Pandora helped tremendously. Korn Radio is my go-to when my melancholia piques. And though I was not tempted to drive into oncoming traffic or find a bridge to leap from, I certainly was feeling rather, well…blue, I guess you could say.

I tried in vain to mimic Jonathan Davis' bevy of incoherent grunts and verbal undulations during *Twist,* just as I had for more than twenty years. I bet I looked ridiculous, should anyone have seen me; but after the morning I had had, ...

I arrived at home to find my wife hard at work scrubbing traces of toothpaste spittle from my side of the bathroom mirror. Never one for small talk, or even lighthearted salutations, Molly did not even turn to face me and said, "So, what'd the doc say?"

"I'm dead."

"Huh. Well. I guess you were right then." And for good measure added another "huh."

"Yeah. Thought I should tell you first. Oh, and here." I tried to hand the book to her.

"Thank you. Just, um, put it over there," as she used her face and forehead to motion toward her half of the sink.

"K."

"K. Love you. Be careful going to work."

"K," I said.

I was sad driving to work, even more depressed and defeated and deflated than usual. Not the kind of sad like when you hear you have cancer or can't have kids, etc., but an altogether different kind of sad. It ran deep, this sadness. I wanted to do much more before I died, not unlike everyone else. And just like the rest, I failed to do so. Oh well. If Vonnegut were here with me, he would sum it up succinctly by saying "so it goes." But Vonnegut is not here. He, too, is dead.

I wonder what he's up to?

Someone had parked in my spot when I arrived at work. Probably that dipshit Donnie. I had to park at the far end of the lot; back where even the security cameras were of no use. We once had security officers patrolling on golf carts, but budget cuts put a halt to that. Doesn't matter. I'm dead anyway. Thieves could pick the old jalopy apart for all I cared. They could even help themselves to the

Bukowski book and my own unfinished manuscript that hid somewhere in the back seat.

After parking my car, I began the long hike to the office. About fifty yards into the walk, however, I turned around and went back for the manuscript. Just in case. Dead men can write bestsellers, too.

I straightened my tie; I tucked in my shirt. And I keyed Donnie's car like a motherfucker.

After the half-mile trek in the August sun I finally reached the office. The air conditioning was busted in the rundown old building, they told me. I shrugged. Couldn't feel that shit anyway. Not in my condition. On a normal day I would have sweat through my wine red Peter Millar shirt; but when I finally reached my little office, the last of thirty or so laid out side-by-side, I was as dry as a popcorn fart. No sweat on my forehead, nor in my pits. For good measure, I thrusted my hand down the front of my pants, and with a scooping motion from butthole to ball-sack, discovered that area to also be *sans* moisture. Hence, I discovered the only advantage of being dead. I found it to be exceptionally bright inside my little makeshift domicile, so standing on my expensive-looking leather chair I hurriedly unscrewed one of the two exposed fluorescent bulbs overhead.

I had just logged in to my computer when Katrina, one of just two receptionists shared by the entire sales staff, stepped in my office and handed to me a large stack of paper.

"What the hell is this now?" I asked.

"New HR manual," she said. "Just updated, hot off the presses."

"Any changes worth noting?"

"Nah. Just a couple new paragraphs about personal conduct outside the office."

I chuckled to myself. "I bet I know why that was added."

"You guessed it: when Arnold was busted blowing that guy in the bookstore crapper new policies had to be in put in place."

"Thanks a hell of a lot, Arnie."

"Yeah," Kat replied. "No kidding."

"Well, thanks anyway. I'll put it in my desk on top of the last one."

"Sounds good." She began to walk away, then turned back to me. "Oh, I almost forgot! What did the doc say?"

"I'm dead."

"Hmm. Well, you were right after all."

"Yep. It sucks always being right."

"Anything you need before I go?" she asked. "Want me to get maintenance to fix your lights?"

"No. Actually, wait, yes! There is something I need: if you see Donnie, tell him he parked in my spot."

"No can do, genius."

"Why not?"

"He's in Arizona." She could tell by my expression that I had forgotten. "Remember? His daughter is getting married."

"Oh. That's right." And I felt bad momentarily.

"Why do you need Donnie anyway?"

"Oh, no reason. Have a good afternoon, Kat."

I got to work right away, making sales calls and pretending everything was okay. All afternoon well-wishers stopped by to say things like "heard the bad news—so sorry," and "hang in there, Champ", and "anything I can do to help?" It was all sweet, and very uncharacteristic; so much so that it almost made me uncomfortable. Somehow.

Around three-thirty Katrina came back and surprised me with a slice of red velvet cake.

"My favorite! Thank you, Kat. This is just what I needed." I inhaled for show, seeing as how I couldn't smell a damn thing. Then I smiled so big it made her absolutely glow.

"No problem, Champ. I know it's your favorite and I know Hyde Park Deli's is the best. Look: I even had them add extra shaved coconut frosting."

And she had. Goddamn…there aren't enough Katrinas in the world.

I tried to offer her money, but she refused. I never kept silverware, or even the plastic facsimiles, in my office; so I devoured the cake holding it like a hamburger. I could not taste it involving the conventional method of taste buds (being dead and all) but I recalled so vividly the taste of red velvet cake with coconut that the end result was just the same. And for a few brief moments I felt good. Almost alive. Red velvet was my dad's favorite, too. And he too is dead.
I wrote myself a reminder note to check in on him some time.

A little after four I received a text from Molly saying I could have saved a couple bucks getting that Reese Witherspoon book across town at Wal-Mart. I know what I wanted to say in reply, but decided to be a gentleman and I let it go. I could return it the next day. Or could I? In my condition, who knew? I felt stupid for buying her a book anyway. Buying a millennial a book is like buying an old man a box of tampons.

A few minutes later Scott, the building manager, stepped in my office and asked if I clogged the shitter on the third floor again. I said no, but suggested it was most likely Donnie. He apologized for interrupting me, and turned to leave after bro-hugging me much too strongly. I assumed he heard the bad news too. He eyed the missing fluorescent overhead, but said nothing and exited. I silently hoped he would not be returning with a replacement bulb. The dimness was pleasing to me.

My co-workers began leaving at five just like always. That was always my favorite time of day. An unusual assortment of these blank faces wished me well, saying things like "hang in there" and to be sure to let them know if they could do anything to help. *Anything to help*. It was almost laughable, if it weren't so damn sweet. People will surprise you sometimes.

The environment grew increasingly quieter. Eventually I knew I was alone there, in the brick building located on the east side of an American city known only for lousy sports teams and unusual chili. I moved my chair to once again climb atop it and unscrew a bulb. The only light was now emanating from the computer on my desk and even that was too much. But I was not ready for total darkness just yet, so I accepted it. I swiveled my ass in the chair to face out my window and away from the door. And I waited for the sun to go down. I waited for the cessation of all things. I waited and was not displeased.

"Christ," I said to absolutely no one. "Who the hell's gonna take that damn book back now?"

The Fluffer

By the time the plane's descent into CVG had begun, her friends had been waiting at the gate for almost two hours. Emma was coming home for a week and oh how they had missed her.

Though her seat was located in the middle of the plane, Emma waited so as to be the last person to depart from it. This homecoming was bittersweet. She knew she would have to answer question after tiresome question about her new life in Los Angeles and she dreaded it. She also dreaded the weather upon looking out her window, and silently she prayed that her assistant remembered to pack her at least one hoodie or rain jacket. When the last passenger had exited the plane, Emma slid on her flip flops, stood and stretched, then removed her duffle bag from the overhead compartment at a pace that could be described with accuracy as sluggish.

She took an extraordinary amount of time navigating the jetway. She powered-up her phone and waited to see any new texts. Indeed, there were a few. Three were from a producer she had worked with several times before, and a fourth was from her assistant Rose telling her to be safe and included a phone number for a doctor in Cincinnati that specializes in TMJ. She replied to neither of them.

Meryl Streep could not have feigned a bigger and brighter smile when Emma's eyes met those of her friends Erica and Kayla. Her sister Heather was also present and was exceedingly pleased to greet her. Emma was appalled that all three had gained a great deal of weight since the last time they all met, some three years prior; but, she knew better than to mention it. They rushed to meet her, embracing her with rib-splintering hugs and covering her cheeks in coffee-flavored kisses. Then endless mind-numbing choruses of "you look so beautiful!", and "you haven't changed a bit," and questions about her health stemming from the unnerving fact that Emma had not gained a single pound since her move to the coast. The rain had begun falling harder the last few minutes, so they, as a group, decided to wait it out in the hotel bar.

Emma was completely on board with this. She knew booze would be her friend these next few days.

The hostess directed the group to a table in the very center of the establishment and poured them each a glass of water. This brought out a sense of the claustrophobia that had plagued Emma since childhood. It was a perfect metaphor, she told herself, of her time spent growing up in the Midwest: the inability to breathe from the world closing in; feeling trapped, and constantly searching for routes to which escape. Heather, her sister, took note of the silence and the sweat beginning to appear on Emma's forehead, which was uncharacteristically free of makeup.

"Well, little sis, tell us all about it. What's life like in LA?"

"And the men! Tell us about the hunks there," chimed-in Kayla.

"And tell us about this Rose girl that's in all your Facebook posts. Are you a lesbian? It's cool if you are. I know lots of lesbians," added Erica. "It's not that big a deal anymore."

"No, I'm not a lesbian," said Emma after a long sip of water and a short laugh.

"See," said Heather. "I told ya. Besides, Erica, she's too skinny to be a lesbian." This brought laughter from group, including Emma, who longed for a waiter to finally appear and take their drink orders. It was shaping-up to be a rum day for sure.

Emma kicked off her shoes and sat Indian-style and listened to the banter, engaging when she had to. She answered their questions about the weather in Los Angeles, the gorgeous people there, the high cost of living, etc. She was explaining the proximity of her apartment in the San Fernando Valley to Hollywood when the waiter arrived. Emma heard him before she saw him; and she immediately recognized the voice.

"Good afternoon, ladies. My name is Kevin. Can I take your drink orders?"

That was when all four of them recognized the clean-cut young man. Erica and Kayla leapt up and hugged him. Heather remained seated, but touched him on the forearm and told him he looks well. Emma barely breathed, as if in a trance, or a nightmare, and her eyes once again began to search for an escape route.

"Hi, Em. You look great. It's been a long time," said Kevin in his deep baritone voice. All eyes turned to look at her, waiting her response.

She smiled, and said "excuse me." She then walked hurriedly to the bathroom without putting on her shoes. She knew this trip was a mistake; and as the tears welled-up in her eyes all she wanted to do was somehow turn back the hands of time and sleep-in, rather than catch that plane at LAX.

The group did not know how to react. Kayla, the loquacious one, suggested that Emma was just air sick and asked Kevin to bring two pitchers of margaritas, heavy on the alcohol, and four glasses. He agreed, and left four menus on the table.

After several minutes one pitcher arrived, but no Emma. Heather agreed to check on her little sister and walked to the bathroom. She saw bare feet under the farthest stall, and lightly approached. She rapped gingerly on the door if it.

"You knew he worked here, didn't you?"

"No. I swear I didn't know, Em. And I'm sorry. We can pay for the drinks and leave if you want."

"Look; it's fine. Just, I don't know, give me a minute, okay?"

"Take all the time you need; but I'm not leaving this bathroom without you."

Emma smiled, just a little, then said, "you sure about that?" And with that, little Emma McDonough, the petite former homecoming queen and the face of Proctor & Gamble's Brilliant White Smile ad campaign ripped a fart. And it was a big one. A fart that a three-hundred-pound trucker would have been proud to call his own. And Heather laughed so hard she almost lost her balance. Emma, too, laughed so boisterously that she snorted; which only caused the two to laugh even harder.

Emma opened the door and hugged her sister.

The pitcher was just one glass away from being empty when Emma finished it off by hoisting the entire cruet and, tilting her head back fully, she downed its contents like a nineteen-year-old at a frat party. Heather and their friends, in awe of this rare spectacle of her inelegance, just stared in slack-jawed astonishment as Emma licked her lips, slammed down the empty amphora and said lightheartedly with intent to induce humor "told you bitches this mouth is still the best in town."

Just as she said this, Kevin approached the table with the food ordered and, once again, Emma felt an uneasy embarrassment. He smiled and pretended he had not heard a thing. One by one, he sat the appropriate plate of food in front of each patron. Emma noticed Erica watching with laser-like focus every bend of Kevin's arm, which caused the vascularity of his forearm to showcase itself prominently. In Emma's line of work, there was no such thing as jealousy. In fact, that was a sure way to get oneself blacklisted in the Valley. So she attempted to shift her focus from her former friend to the beautifully blackened salmon in front of her.

Everyone began eating, with exception of Erica. Rather than a knife or fork, the tool she wielded was her smart phone.

"What are you doing?" Kayla asked her.

"Who? Me? Oh, I'm just doing a little recon work, that's all." Erica said this with a grin belying a secret she simultaneously longed to tell and longed not to. Heather and Kayla, who flanked her on either side, leaned in for a closer look.

"There! Found him," Erica said triumphantly. And added for good measure, "relationship status: unconfirmed." She pulled the phone closer to her nose, as if that would change what the profile of Kevin Woods read. "Uncomfirmed? What the hell does that even mean?"

Perhaps sensing that the subject matter could be potentially upsetting to their guest, Heather chimed in suggesting that Erica put her phone away and enjoy their time together; the four of them, just as they did in high school. Terribly bemused and dreadfully incapable of reading the room, Erica sat her phone beside her plate and scrolled with her dominant right hand, holding her fork discommodiously in her left. Emma, just as she did as a child, pulled her knee up to her chest and hid her face behind it while picking at her salmon with a knife. Heather and Kayla ate their steaks with gusto, both either oblivious to, or completely ignoring, the growing uncomfortableness around them.

"So, Em, tell us what you do now," said Kayla. "I mean, we know you work on film sets. Do you do hair and makeup? Or is it catering?"

"Or maybe a script supervisor? I always thought that would be fun," added Heather.

Emma thought about how best to answer, then swallowed a small bite of salmon. "Well, I guess you could say, it's a little of all of that." She said this without sounding cagey, which she rehearsed and prepared for on the plane.

"Oh wow," Kayla replied enthusiastically. "Is that why you have an assistant? Because you're having to do so many things all the time?"

"Yeah. Pretty much." As she said this, Emma felt her phone vibrate. She pulled it from her back pocket and read the text silently. It was from Rose. She said that Sidney, the girl replacing her on set Monday, now has a cold sore and cannot perform, and asked if she can return from Ohio a day early. Emma did not know how to answer, so she chose not to. She would reply when she felt like talking about work.

"How come you're not on IMDB?"

Emma looked at Erica with a blank expression, unsure of how to answer her. She picked at loose skin around her left thumbnail as she felt three pairs of eyes staring deep into her.

"I don't know. I just, I don't know, just want to get my money and go home when the day is done. I don't much care about getting the credits."

This answer seemed to placate the crowd; Heather specifically, who noted that their father was also one to never take credit when credit was due. "See, ladies, that is good Catholic humility." She smiled and raised a glass of margarita to her little sister, as did Kayla.

Erica was still engrossed in her phone.

"Have you worked on any sets with big stars? Names we might recognize," asked Kayla.

"Well, Emma began, "Tobey Maguire likes to hang out sometimes on some of the sets where I work."

This revelation was enough to even bring Erica back into the real world.

"Tobey Maguire? As in *Seabiscuit*, Tobey Maguire? *The Great Gatsby*, Tobey Maguire?"

Emma smiled and nodded her head. This made the others swoon as if the Hollywood A-lister himself had graced their table.

"Oh I love him!" "Oh I do, too!" "I have *always* loved little Tobey!"

"Yeah, and one day, Dax Shepard and Kristen Bell showed up on set, just out of the blue."

"Oh my God, that is spectacular! Did you get a picture with them?" asked Kayla. The other two turned their faces to Emma, hoping for a response in the affirmative.

Emma bought time by swallowing another small bite of salmon. "Um, no. I can't really do that on set. It's kind of, you know, frowned upon." The three nodded, suggesting they indeed understood film set decorum. Even if that film happened to be of pornographic nature. Fortunately, Emma had been able to maintain secrecy regarding the only genre of film she could seem to book.

"But it's okay. I still get to meet so many nice people. And they're always gracious. And I get paid daily. That's the best part."

"Daily?" Erica seemed vexed by this statement. "Em," saying with obviously intended insolence, "it sounds like you make porn, not indie flicks." Erica laughed, finding herself hilarious just as she always had. Heather and Kayla laughed as well, and the former waved slightly to Kevin, then pointed to the empty pitcher, letting him know to bring another. Emma's eyes met Erica's. *Did she know?* Emma wondered. But she knew the chances of that were slim. Emma had only been in front of the camera on one adult film set, eight years ago, shortly after arriving in LA. And as far as she knew, only one person from her hometown, and from her former life, knew about that. And she visibly shivered when she recalled the visage of that man, and the ugly aftermath of his being made aware. Since then, her new career was one hundred percent behind the lens.

Emma's phone rang as Kevin, with the sleeves of his shirt now rolled up one fold higher on his muscular arm, provided the table with their second pitcher. It was Rose calling, her young and unblemished twenty-four-year-old face making fish lips filled the entirety of the screen. Emma momentarily admired Rose's contact photo, her reddish hair and bright red lips and wondered, for the first time, if Rose was her real first name. She swiped the red X, sending the call to voice mail as Heather filled all four glasses with the green slushy panty-remover, and Erica took her eyes off her phone long enough to notice that Kevin's ring finger was free of adornment, but a tan line where a ring was sometimes worn showed itself. She rolled her eyes at this and turned her phone face-side down in frustration. Kayla stole a forkful of salmon from Emma's plate and shoved it in her mouth, uncaring of anything around her or even the basest of dining decorum.

Kevin looked longingly at Emma. Emma looked at the floor.

"Well, ladies, my shift is almost up so I'm going to leave these with you," and Kevin placed the checks beside the plates of each of them. "I'm still on for a few, so if you need anything or want me to get these plates out of your way, just holler."

Emma cringed at "just holler." She hadn't always; in fact, she once found it quite adorable when his hillbilly lineage showed itself. But those days were well in the past.

Heather asked if he could begin clearing the plates, and Kayla stole another bite from Emma before it was too late. Erica eyed her check strangely, but said nothing. Emma offered to pay for the group, since the week would be spent crashing with each of them and interrupting their lives their somewhat. Erica and Heather complied, but put up false fights in doing so. Erica kept a tight grip on her ticket and thanked Emma for the kind offer, but she would pay for her own food. The group decided against leaving right away; the booze suggested they should wait it out for a while longer. Besides, the rain began falling harder than before. Erica gave Kevin a debit card and Emma gave hers to Heather to pass to him.

Emma's phone rang again; and once again, the face of her assistant was screaming at her two-dimensionally. Tempted again to send the call to voice mail, she excused herself and walked hurriedly out of the restaurant and into the airport, again without putting on her shoes. From where they sat, Heather, Kayla, and Erica could see through the large window separating and isolating the two worlds.

"Hello."

"Em, hi, it's Rose. Did you get my message?"

"No, not yet. I'm kind of busy catching up, you know? I told you I'm trying to go off the grid for a week."

"Yeah, I know, but listen: Bacchus called, he and his crew are coming to LA and he asked for you by name. Said he'll add five Benjamins to your daily rate."

Emma did not immediately answer. She knew that a producer of Bacchus's caliber asking for her by name would be career suicide if she refused. But she needed a break. Physically and mentally she was exhausted. Besides, her jaw hurt like a bitch and she needed to see the specialist in town that Rose had found online and vetted for her.

"Hello? Em, you there?"

"Yes, sorry, I'm here. Just thinking." But she was not thinking about flying back so quickly, as Rose would hope. She instead was thinking of the perfect excuse to get out of this situation; one that would allow her to save face and continue her career while still allowing herself to once again be Emma McNobody from Nowhere, Ohio for a little while.

"Well, Bacchus needs to know. Like, now." And of course he did; all producers claimed to need to know *like now*. That was one of the most overused idioms in an industry fraught with overused idioms. Emma needed to bide more time; to weigh the pros and cons of saying no to an adult industry heavyweight.

"Who would I be working with? Do you know the males that have been cast?"

"Only dude mentioned," replied Rose, "was Apollo." This was followed by another bout of silence. Emma peered over her shoulder and inside the restaurant her friends watched her pace back and forth, barefoot, with her phone pressed to her face. Time was slowing for her; even though hundreds of people walked by her in such a rush that it seemed that the world was ending.

"Okay, Em you gotta stop leaving me hanging like that."

"I know, I'm sorry. Look: can you do it? I know it's been a while, but there's nothing to it."

Emma knew the answer to this. Rose had been a fluffer before, though quite briefly. It was on her third film set, just two years ago when she was flat-chested and just off the bus from Rock Valley, Iowa, that she discovered a new career path was in her best interest. Not coincidentally, that was the day she met the aforementioned Apollo.

"You know I can't. Even if I wanted to, which I don't, Apollo won't work with me again. Last time I made him bleed. I told you about that remember? My mouth can only open so far. And my stupid tooth caught him in the worst spot. I thought they were going to kill me, Em. They couldn't film until he healed."

"Oh come on, Love, I'm sure he doesn't even remember that." Emma did not believe the words she just spoke, but wanted to very badly. Leaned against the thick front glass separating the serenity of the restaurant from the chaos of a Midwest airport, she placed one arm across her chest, allowing her other arm to hold the phone tightly to ear; and she thanked God she switched to sports bras exclusively.

Inside the restaurant, the debit cards were returned with receipts to be signed. Erica autographed hers with a large bold heart dotting the *i* in her name. Though her three lunch companions were no longer watching Emma, someone else was.

Kevin stood beside the bar, some twenty feet away from the table he waited earlier, and now off the clock watched every move his former sweetheart made. Through the glass he could hear nothing, so he tried to read her lips. He was able to make out "flight," and "LA," and "cock." She was still the most beautiful girl he had ever laid eyes on. His phone vibrated in his pocket, just inches away from his blooming erection, but he chose to ignore the incoming text. His mind wandered to the good times, back to when they, he and Emma, met at community college and to their first date: A Reds game. It was her idea, he reminded himself, seeing as how they met in an accounting class both sporting a Ken Griffey, Jr. jersey. Had it really been a decade ago? he asked himself. Indeed, it had; and in some ways it felt longer.

His phone vibrated again, signaling another incoming text. This time, he removed the phone from his pocket. The text was from a number not in his list of contacts. The first text, the one he ignored, read "sup sexy? Thanks for writing your number on my check." It was followed by a kissy face emoji.

The second text, from the same number, was a jpeg. A black-haired woman, about thirty years old, topless before a changing room mirror. One arm was strategically placed to hide the area of the stomach just below the naval and above the pants often called the FUPA. Kevin looked up from his phone to see Erica looking at him seductively from her chair; then she placed the straw from her glass of water in her mouth, little by little taking it further in, not breaking eye contact with him. Kevin sheepishly smiled back and added the number to his list of contacts under the name "Emsfriend."

"Erica! Stop that," demanded Heather. "You haven't seen Emma in three years and you're flirting with her ex?"

"Yeah…ex," replied Erica. "That's the key word here: ex."

"Yeah I know it's her ex," interjected Kayla, oblivious to the black pepper lodged between several of her teeth. "But come on, Erica: this is Em we're talking about. You know how in love with him she was."

"Yeah…was."

"Dammit, Erica."

"What? What's the big deal, Heather? She got all the hot guys in high school and she's probably swimming in dicks in LA. But I'm not allowed to have a little fun?"
Heather and Kayla did not know how to reply. They knew what Erica was saying was right, so maybe they were being too hard on her.

"Look," Erica continued, "I'm a month away from thirty. I have no kids, no husband anymore, and I stay so wet that I slide off my goddamn furniture. So yeah, if he's up for it, I'm taking that man home tonight." Then, biting her lip, she mumbled something about being glad she shaved her biscuit that morning.

Kayla looked at Heather. "Speaking of 'up for it,' didn't Emma once say that Kevin is, you know…swinging a bat down there?"

Heather, taking a drink of her margarita, almost shot it right back out through her nostrils. She laughed, as did the other two, then replied, "yes, I heard my sister say that more than once."
The collective eyes of the triumvirate then turned to their waiter, now sitting on a barstool, looking out the front window. This time, however, their gazes shifted from the arms, down to the crotch; and each imagined what was hiding beneath those black Dockers.

"Lord, forgive me," Heather said, caressing the crucifix below her chins and trying to calm her breathing.

Kayla added, "this was a bad year to give up masturbation for Lent."

"Of course he remembers it! Here, Em, allow me to paint you a picture. Imagine if you will, a large African-American adult film star--we'll call him 'Apollo'--with a dick the size of grandad's thermos. And now imagine a fair maiden, *moi*, being tasked with the job of keeping said penis erect..."

Emma found Rose unbearably cute when she talked like this; and she muffled her giggles in her free hand.

"...but I failed so greatly that production had to be postponed; and Bacchus himself threatened to punch my teeth out. Which, in hindsight, might have worked out well for me in the end."

"Stop. Don't even kid about that!" Emma's hand was now clenched in uncharacteristic fury as she pictured what Rose had to go through that day because of a simple mistake. She knew that porn sets are full of dangerous testosterone; and testosterone is flammable in bulk. There are no unions for fellatists, professional or amateur. Bacchus outweighed Rose by a hundred pounds, and every ounce of that was solid muscle. And Apollo outweighed Bacchus by twenty-five or thirty. Yes, they could have killed her assistant that day and no one would have missed her. There are no headlines when a fluffer goes missing or is beaten to death. No candlelight vigils when even the sweetest of these nameless and faceless oral artists goes to sleep for the last time. Emma's mind was made up.

"Tell Bacchus I said no thanks."

"Emma, please think this through. You're my boss, so I will do as you say; but they're adding five hundred on top of your normal per diem. Plus, and let's not forget about this, they could blacklist you just the same as they did to me. You're twenty-nine years old, and you are, in every producer and actor's opinion, the best at what you do."

"Christ, Rose; you make me sound like an accountant. Or a hitman."

"Ugh. Take the compliment, you big c-word."

This made Emma laugh so hard that she accidentally kicked the glass behind her, startling the patrons on the other side.

"Okay, sluts, what are we doing next?" asked Emma as she returned to the table, resting a knee on her chair rather than sitting in it.

"Well someone is in a good mood all of a sudden," said Kayla.

"Yeah," Heather agreed. "Who was that on the phone? Gosling? Clooney?"

"Even hotter: Danny DeVito," replied Emma. "Thanking me for the threesome with Steve Buscemi."

"Well...I just lost my ladyboner; anyone else?" asked Kayla, stuffing her phone in her bra and taking one last gulp from her glass of water. Erica and Heather nodded in affirmation.

"I booked mani-pedis for the four of us at the Asian salon in Hyde Park. I figured we could do that to lose our buzz and chill before going to Erica's for shitty-movie night."

"Sounds absolutely perfect, big sis!" Emma exclaimed. She looked at the chipped paint on her fingers, then her toes while sliding them into her flip flops. "I'm thinking fuchsia."

"You ladies go ahead. I'll meet you at the car. I gotta hit the poop-closet."

"Gross, Erica, but okay," retorted Heather, rolling her eyes. They grabbed their belongings and Kayla left a twenty-dollar cash tip on the table. Heather shouted goodbye to Kevin; Kayla waved to him and Emma sheepishly smiled and nodded to him; he replied in kind.

Though the rain had stopped falling so hard, there was still a drizzle as the group, minus one, scurried to Heather's minivan, located in short-term parking. Emma, substantially lighter than her sister and friend, ran ahead of them; at one point gleefully turning to face them and shouting "shotgun!"

"You bitch!" Kayla screamed back laughingly.

Arriving at the van, Heather had to dig deeply in her purse to find the key. Once she did, they climbed inside and cranked the heat to get warm. Emma, seated in her rightfully-called spot (the passenger seat) unzipped her duffle bag and found the thick blue Disneyland hoodie Rose had packed for her. She hurriedly peeled the rain-soaked white tee shirt she had been donning all day and put on the hoodie, zipping it all the way to her chin. She then removed her phone from her back pocket and took a selfie; her new favorite article of clothing being more prominently displayed than her face. Emma then texted the selfie to Rose, along with the words, "thank you Love." Within seconds she received Rose's reply: "yw, c word" followed by an emoji of a fat yellow winking face with its tongue stuck out.

Kayla, relegated to the backseat, was taking inventory of Heather's DVD collection. "Christ, Heather, all you have is Disney."

"Yeah, ho; I have two kids, remember?"

"Yeah, I know, but holy hell… is it too much to ask to have one copy of *Magic Mike* for occasions like this?"

"Kayla, there will be no bean-flicking in my sister's car, *comprende?*"

"Well, to be fair," Heather interjected, "no one other than yours truly will be bean-flicking in this car."

"Eww. Coulda done without hearing that."

Heather and Kayla laughed. "Hey, little sis, running from the airport just now was the most cardio I've done since Rick got his promotion; if you catch my drift."

"Duly noted. And still eww."

Kayla was eyeing the shrewdly-hidden golden phalluses on the cover of *The Little Mermaid* when her phone vibrated in her bra. Removing it with the grace of an old-timey detective removing his pistol from a shoulder holster, she entered her passcode and opened the message. "Hmm, well that didn't take long," she said shoving the hefty teat back in its place.

Heather, adjusting her rearview mirror to see Kayla better, asked "what do you mean?"

"Oh, just this." She turned the phone so it faced Emma and Heather. And what they saw was an image; the sender was Erica. It was a selfie of Erica in the ladies' room of the restaurant they just left, on her knees, staring doe-eyed into the camera, with a fat, veiny penis in her mouth. Well, not *in* her mouth, exactly; but rather across it, like a fleshy, vascular harmonica; or a Salvador Dali mustache.

Heather, rolling her eyes and not connecting the dots, asked to whom the penis was attached.

Then the awful realization hit her, and she turned to face her sister. "Em, I'm so sorry. I wouldn't have asked her to come if I knew ..."

"Look, it's fine. I don't even care," Emma said, feigning a smile. "I've moved on to bigger and better things. And by *things* I mean *dicks*." She laughed when she said this, hoping it would be infectious enough for the others to laugh, too. A noble attempt, but a failed one.

"Em, I feel terrible," said Kayla. "I shouldn't have shown you that. I'm so sorry." And she was; Emma knew this. Though her head was reeling from all the conflicting emotions running through it, none of them involved hating Kayla. Time and distance had softened old wounds; but, unfortunately, not killed them.

"He has weird balls," added Heather.

The three sat in awkward silence. Kayla studied her phone, taking in each pixel before having to delete the picture, for fear of her husband seeing it. Heather nervously searched through XM radio stations, never settling on one for more than a few seconds. Emma was statuesque, obviously in deep contemplation.

Some homecoming.

The silence was too much to bear, and it added to the frustration that had been building inside her since she landed. Emma determined at that moment to make this trip memorable, for better or worse. She slid her flip flops back on her feet.

"I'm going inside. Be back in a minute." Before the others could protest, Emma had opened the door and was sprinting to the airport entrance.

"Oh shit," said Kayla. "Should we warn Erica?"

"Nope," replied Heather sternly. "She's got this coming to her."

Emma looked a mess as she navigated the long, taupe-colored hallways of CVG. Her hair was soaked and every step produced a mind-numbing squish sound from her five-year-old flip flops. After a couple hundred yards of suffering through this horrendous sonance she kicked them off once again, choosing to carry them in her right hand.

Approaching she entrance, she bumped into Erica—literally, just inside the airport.

"Emma!" she exclaimed. "what are you doing here?" Her eyes were alarmed, practically bulging out of their sockets. She was afraid; fearful of a potentially humiliating scene that could commence at any moment.

"Follow me," Emma said while grabbing her friend by the arm with her free hand. "Not a word; you let me do the talking."

To neither's surprise, they found Kevin exactly where he was when Erica left his presence: sitting at the bar, scrolling through the gallery of his phone. He was visibly filled with dread when approached by the duo. He hadn't the time to even put his phone away before Emma sat her soaked flip flops on the bar and, with her nose mere inches from his, asked a question he was unprepared to answer.

"What's her name?" Emma inquired.

"Huh? Who?"

Mocking him as if he possessed mental deficiencies, she repeated his *huh* and *who*. Then she repeated her original question, but this time pointing to Erica. "What's her name?" Emma was unflinching; spine snapped arrow-straight and eyes ablaze.

Kevin struggled to find the answer. His eyes shifted, up and to the left, hoping something—anything—would jog his memory. No answer came. His mouth hung slack, not unlike a teenage boy attempting to locate the clitoris. Erica was also at a loss for words.

"Farrah," said Emma. "Her name is Farrah."

"Farrah!" Kevin exclaimed proudly. "I knew it was Farr…"

The slap across the face came so quickly that it caught even Erica off guard. And the sound of it was similar to that of a single-barrel shotgun's report. "It's Erica, you dipshit. Her name is Erica!"

With tears of shame welling in his eyes Kevin looked about the place, to see just how many people had witnessed his comeuppance. Erica's hand covered her open mouth; she was rendered speechless, for perhaps the first time in her life. She left, backing away slowly at first, then turning to sprint, still covering her face in embarrassment.

There were only a handful of patrons in the restaurant at the time. None of them witnessed the slap, but each heard it. And each set of eyes was now fixed upon the former lovers and their heated exchange. Kevin grabbed Emma by the arm and led her to a quieter and less visible locale, the area behind the bar that led to the restrooms. Even though he was technically off the clock, he was afraid of being fired.

"Stop! You're going to get my ass terminated!" he said, grabbing Emma by the shoulders, tears still forming in his reddened eyes.

"No, you don't get to tell me what to do. Not anymore" she snapped back, violently removing his hands from her. "So some things never change, do they? Still the same Kevin. Kevin that can sniff out weakness and vulnerability and pounce on it like a goddamn hyena."

"Okay. Calm the fuck down. What is your deal? This is none of your business. If your friend…"

"…Erica."

"Yes, Erica—if she wants to go down on someone that's her business. She's over eighteen. She made the decision and I didn't force her…"

"Oh spare me that shit! You sat at the bar when your shift was finished just looking for the right girl. No! Wait…not the *right* girl. But the easy one. The low-hanging fruit. The one that is just the right age and with low enough standards to get you off without having to even learn her fucking name."

She was right, and he knew that. But he was also right: he did not have to explain himself, and knowing this steeled his spine.

"Well, you certainly have room to talk" he said with a dickish and coy grin. "Are you sure you really want to get into a conversation about anonymous blowjobs here?"

The second slap to his face came even quicker than the first.

"Dammit, Em…stop hitting me!"

"You want mercy? After all the shit you put me through? Need I remind you of everything that transpired between us, assface?" The sound of Kevin's cheek being bashed was heard by several people, including the aged and barely mobile restaurant manager, who came around the corner in a hurry to find the pair.

"Kevin…is everything alright here?"

Kevin tried to smile and laugh a little, shaking off the whole situation as a joke. "Yeah, Barry, everything is copacetic here. Just catching up with an old friend." He smiled at Emma. Emma stared into his eyes and mouthed silently "fuck…you."

Barry, exercising his extensive managerial training and intuition asked her "you okay, ma'am?"

"Yep, Bare—can I call you Bare? —me and ol' Kev here were just discussing a blowjob." She smiled at Barry. Barry, in shock, looked to his young waiter, whose mouth had dropped wide open; then, regathering himself, laughed like a schoolboy that got caught rubbing one out.

"She…um, she's a kidder, Barry. Just a big kidder."

Barry looked disapprovingly and said "well, once you're finished here, swing by my office. We need to talk."

"Will do, Boss." Barry disappeared around the corner.

"Jesus Christ, Em! Are you happy now? I could get fired!"

"Oh! I'm so sorry! I would hate to sabotage the career of a waiter hanging around an airport bar after his shift ends to get unprotected head. Let me guess: that's your M.O., isn't it? Flirting with a table of middle aged muffin tops knowing that one of them will certainly take the bait. Was she even the first one today?"

Kevin grabbed her arm and dragged her toward the ladies' room. Emma did not put up a fight, only voicing her concern about her unattended flip flops. He assured her that if they were to be stolen while they talked that he would purchase new ones for her. She acquiesced and walked peacefully beside him, shaking off his attempt to hold her hand.

"Should we check on them? They've been gone a while," Kayla asked, hoping Heather was listening.

"No. I'm sure we'll hear all about it soon enough."

"About the blowjob?"

"No! Well, yes…but I meant after that. I just hope they're not fighting."

"Me too. But if they are, I've got fifty bucks on my sister. Emma knows how to use her fists. She's a born fighter."

Kayla smiled. "Well I've heard that's just one way of using her hands that she excels at."

Heather, perplexed, twisted her neckless body as well as she could and asked "what do you mean?" She honestly didn't know.

"It's a little late to be jealous, don't ya think?"

"Jealous? Okay, let's get one thing straight here: I care nothing for you. I haven't for a very long time. What I do care about, you pompous ass, is my friend. If you would have told me her name when I asked you, I would've walked away quietly. Stop treating people like they're disposable!"

They stood about a foot apart, Kevin with his back against the door. He lifted weights regularly, so his two hundred pounds would easily prevent someone from entering into their private conversation.

"Okay, I get it: I'm an asshole. But what do you care? Aren't you still in LA? Besides, don't think for a second that I don't know what you do out there." He braced himself for another blow, but it didn't come.

"Fair enough...I'll bite. What is it that I do out there?"

He cocked an eyebrow. "Oh come on...don't make me say it." Emma folded her arms across her chest and gave him a look as if saying *go ahead...I'm waiting*. "You're a porn star," he said.

Visibly relieved, as if a weight had been lifted, Emma sighed deeply and looked down at her feet. She was unsure of how to answer, but she had no qualms about setting the record straight. "Listen," she began, still not looking at him, "I don't owe you an explanation for anything. You or anyone. But if you want to have this conversation, I'll have it. No...I'm no porn star. I assume, by you mentioning it, you saw a video..."

"The casting couch," Kevin interrupted.

"Yes. Fine. The casting couch." She looked up at him, unblinkingly; she could finally be strong around the man that once terrified her greatly. "After we split, I took my one suitcase and my black eye and I went to California. I had a cousin there who said I could split the rent and sleep on her futon until I could afford my own place. The auditions for tv and film were everywhere, until they weren't."

"Why didn't you wait for me? I was going to get a tryout in the minors."

"Bullshit."

"Bullshit? Fuck you! I was good."

"Good? You were a five-eleven first baseman who batted two-ninety-nine and an OBP of three-eleven in junior college!"

"Four-sixteen and five-ninety that summer."

"You were moved to the four-spot and you got lucky with the pitches."

She flinched as his heavy right fist punched the white tile wall behind her, mere inches from her head. But she did not cry.

"And you're a righty...scouts look for southpaws in JC." Then adding for good measure "and you swing at everything."

"No. No, I don't believe it" Heather said with absolute certainty. Whomever told you that is a liar."

"Just telling you what I heard," replied Kayla. And it wasn't just Bree...I heard it from Sam too."

"Who?"

"Sam," Kayla repeated. "You know: the tranny that cuts my hair."

"A very reputable source."

"Whoa! When did you get all 'phobic?"

"Oh please," Heather snapped back. "I don't give a shit what is between her legs. I'm talking about her history of meth. And besides, it was *you* that used the word 'tranny.'"

"Oh...shit. My bad" Kayla said, passively admitting to rushing to judgment, as good SJW's often do. "Still...I think it's Emma on that casting couch."

"If you think you are still capable of scaring me or intimidating me, little man, you're dead wrong."

Kevin's eyes were on fire, and staring deep into Emma's with obvious contempt. But she did not cower, she was unfazed, and he knew not how to react to that. The shift in their relationship with one another was near Seismic. Once upon a time, only a few years but also a lifetime ago, little Emma McDonough was determined to please and never offend the boyfriend she loved so dearly. She was unaware, back then, of the now-obvious mental manipulations he exercised on her daily. She just knew that he was handsome and had goals; and that he was wanted by most of the other females at

Habsburg Community College. He made her feel fortunate to possess him.

The knuckles of his right fist were still pressed against the tile when he felt someone trying to enter through the heavy wooden door against his back. "Closed for cleaning!" Kevin shouted, regaining his composure.

"That was quick," Emma said. "That must be your go-to."

"Everyday."

"You're pathetic."

"As are you, Fluffer." As Kevin said this, he readied the left side of his face for another strike. But the strike did not come. Rather, his comment brought a rather grandiose smile to Emma's calm and perfect face. That smiled turned into a laugh, a hearty one. "Well…" he continued, "are you going to deny it? Are you going to pretend that I'm wrong?"

Emma's laugh returned to its original shit-eating grin. "Am I going to deny? Am I going to pretend? No. No I am not. Because I am not ashamed of who I am—not anymore. Who I am ashamed of is the girl I used to be. The girl who took your slaps and your name-calling because you're nothing more than an insecure little momma's boy. Yes, I am a fluffer…and a damn good one. I make your annual salary by tax day working a fraction of the hours."

The comment about the money returned the scowl to Kevin's face. He was experiencing what is frequently called "butthurt."

She continued her long overdue diatribe at his expense. "And I am the best as what I do. Can you say the same, little boy? No, you cannot. Because you are not the best waiter. You're probably not even the best waiter at this shitty airport bar. You're not the best athlete, as we have discussed; and you're not even the best at hiding your relationship." She looked at the ring finger on his left hand, now placed casually, but at-the-ready, on his left hip. The tan line from a wedding ring seemed to shine like a mirage in the desert. He noticed her gaze, and stuck in his hand in his pocket.

"You finished, bitch?"

"Almost. I'd just like to point out the obvious difference between you and I."

"Which is?' he asked through gritted teeth. His arm still extended just to the right of her face, his knuckles still against the wall.

"Yes, I know what my job is. And I know I choose it. I choose everything I do or do not do. And I choose to be behind the scenes…and therein lies the difference: I choose obscurity; you *are* obscurity." Upon saying this, Emma swiftly used her right hand to strike Kevin's forearm, causing it to give way and his face to plow into the white tile of the wall behind her. His full weight now on her, she shoved him back. He nursed his bruised face with both hands. He said nothing; perhaps quietly soothing his bruised ego as well. "You take care, Kevin. And grow up. Your family deserves better."

She opened the door, shoving him aside, leaving Kevin to rub his face in solitude. Walking briskly, she recovered her flip flops from the bar and put them on her feet. As she was about to exit the establishment she passed the manager, Barry, his arms full with menus and silverware and gave him a little love-tap on his crotch. "Later, Bare!" she said to him without breaking stride.

Erica was sitting near the fountain nearest the airport exit. She saw Emma walking her way and immediately jumped to her feet, her hands folded in shame at her stomach, her eyes just barely high enough to see. "Em…I don't know what to say. I'm so sorry. Please don't hate me." She had been crying.

As Emma approached, she held up one finger and silently mouthed "one second" to her friend. Erica nodded, and Emma removed her phone from her back pocket. She called the last number in her list of recent calls. Rose answered.

"Hey, Em. What's shaking?"

"Not much, Love. What are you doing right now?" Emma paced; Erica remained a statue.

"Eh, just sorting my dildos. You?"

"Sorting them? Like how? By size? By frequency of use?" Emma just had to know.

"No. Well, kind of, maybe" was Rose's reply. I'm sorting by favorite.

"Oh. Well then…who's batting at the top of the order?"

"That's the problem: I'm stuck deciding between Big Luther and 1994 Keanu." As she said this with her phone resting between her cheek and shoulder, Rose had a large black rubber phallus in her left hand, and a smaller, lighter-hued one in her right. "Your thoughts?"

"Big Luther. All day" was Emma's answer. "So listen…I need you to do something. You still have my AMEX, right?" She did not give Rose time enough to answer before continuing. "Book a flight…you're coming to Ohio."

"I am?"

"Indeed. Pack a bag. I need you here."

"You do? Why?" Rose was honestly puzzled. After all, she was simply an assistant.

"Why? Because you're my friend. And my other friends are here. And I want some time with all of you. Actually, I *need* some time with all of you. So pack a bag, throw 1994 Keanu in your purse, and get here tonight, if possible."

"Well, okay then. I'll do that now, if you're sure." Then added "what about Bacchus?"

"Don't worry about Bacchus; I'll call him myself and make everything right."

"Well, okay. I'll pack and text you the flight details. Mwah."

"Mwah back," Emma said before hanging up. She then returned her attention to her long-time friend, who was still standing in the same place, making sparse eye contact, apparently in fear of what may transpire.

"Em, I'm sorry. Please don't hate me."

"Hate you? No, sweetie…not even close. I promise."

"Wow. Really? Are you being serious?"

"Serious as can be. So relax. In fact, how would you like a job?"

Don't Mind Me

It was not the first shrink's office I had found myself in, but it was certainly the nicest. I guess that when one is forty he can afford nicer bullshit therapy sessions than he could at thirty. But I was going to make the most of it, this little game; if only for the benefit of my wife and daughter, whom I love very much. For it was at their urging that I booked an appointment with the most sought-after shrink in the richest part of town.

I never liked coming to Indian Hill. It reminded me that I should have accomplished more in my life; the one and only one I would ever have. The mansions here are less homes and more big taunting bullies. This one calls me "loser" and that one calls me "dipshit," and so on. And every Lexus and Infiniti I met on the roads, driven by ageless wives with no jobs and paid for by husbands with important ones, are just rolling billboards. Billboards that say "vote Republican," and "I'd rather have my tiny dick and big bank account than your big hog and meager savings." And they were right. What's the point of pleasing a woman for an hour or a year when she could have a black AMEX instead? What's the point of ladling soup at a shelter when you could be planning your second Mediterranean before Christmas? I had not been able to take my family on a cruise yet; and they deserved one. They deserved ten. They deserve.

His office was inside a stand-alone red brick building larger than my old high school. He, Cecil Derrick, occupied the first floor. Yes, the entire first floor. I entered the door with trepidation, wearing my new pair of Thursday boots, and new blue corduroy sport coat over a crisp, white dress shirt. All the sartorial channels I followed on YouTube suggested a knot no larger than a four-in-hand if donning a knit tie; but, I felt it was a half-Windsor occasion. To my nervous stomach's dismay, I held my farts all morning, so as not to sully the new dark indigo Gap jeans with putrid ass air.

I looked good, is what I am trying to say. Like a chubby Antonio Centeno.

The walls lining the long hallway were painted a very soothing light green. No pictures were hung, which took me by surprise. Along the drive I had imagined the location to be one big commercial highlighting his own success. Doctor Derrick had, after all, been the one to convince Peter Frampton to pick up his guitar again. And local lore had it that he was the one to convince two Cincinnati Bengals legends to hang up their pads before the undiagnosed CTE worsened and, therefore, saved their lives and perhaps the lives of those closest to them.

After getting lost in the dazzling white maze of the windowless and picture-free hallway I finally made it to the desk of his assistant. The place was practically a warehouse. She, the doctor's assistant, was either forty and looked twenty-seven, or twenty-seven and looked forty. It was hard to tell. Her smile showed teeth so white and straight that I was immediately self-conscious.

"Hello," she said.

"Hello."

"You must be Mister Pot."

"I am. But please, call me Alyosha. Or Al, if you wish. I hope I'm not too early." And I was. I always was. At least half an hour, typically.

"No, you're fine." She reached into her top drawer and drew out a clipboard. On the clipboard was one piece of paper. On this piece of paper were three lines: one for name; one for insurance provider; and the last was a question, one that struck me as odd. The question asked "if you could travel back in time, who is the one person you would fistfight?" And instantly, I liked Dr. Derrick. And instantly, I took the pen out of my pocket and wrote "James Joyce" in the last line. I then wrote my name on the first line and "Anthem" on the second.

After handing the clipboard back to her, Sarah, I learned was her name, I took a seat in a plush red velvet chair in the waiting room directly across from her desk. Nervously using my ring finger to pick at the skin around my left thumb, I took in my surroundings. The scale of the waiting area was quite impressive. The walls were eggshell white and completely bare, except for two large hand-painted and professionally-drawn murals. One I immediately recognized as the logo of the Cincinnati Reds; the other, upon closer inspection, was the crest of Cornell University, the shrink's alma mater. In one of two rich, lush chairs meant for the bottoms of important people, I guessed Sarah to be a good fifty feet away. There was even a grand piano almost within arm's length of where I sat. It too was eggshell white.

"Sixty feet, six inches," she shouted to me.

"Pardon?"

"Sixty and a half feet! You know, like the distance from the pitcher to the catcher!" she screamed even more loudly. "Dr. Derrick loves his baseball!"

It was as if she read my mind. I just smiled politely rather than scream back. How did she know what I was thinking? And how pretentious was it that a man would go to such lengths– twenty yards and change–to isolate his patients from his assistant? I was back to not liking Cecil Derrick.

I had nodded off in the chair, apparently. I awoke to a very tall, very professional-looking gentleman standing over my left shoulder and saying my name. Despite absent-mindedly wiping the drool from my mouth with my right hand, Dr. Derrick still wanted to shake it. I accepted and before he released his grip he asked me to follow him into his office. I tried not to make eye contact with the ambiguously-aged receptionist when I passed her desk, though I do not know why. I found her to be quite warm and accommodating; it was *my* foibles surfacing, not hers.

I tried to match the doctor's ample stride on the way to his office; but, at his height of six-six—I calculated him to be—it was almost impossible. His office was approximately the size of my entire basement, and had minimal furniture—also similar to my basement. There was his grand oak desk, almost reddish in color, with high-back tan leather chair; another tan leather chair facing the doctor's; and a large leather couch placed against a window that I immediately identified as a VIG Chesterfield on the east side of the building. That couch was more valuable than my car.

Dr. Derrick looked more Hollywood than Ohio. His great height was amplified by his choice of shirt: a light blue dress shirt with French cuffs and white vertical stripes. His cuff links were personalized and sterling silver. The Doctor's red silk tie had a small repeating pattern of light blue, but the pattern itself was too small for me to identify at first; then I recognized it to be the Gucci Running logo. His charcoal suspenders matched his pants. The shoes, I noticed while following him to his office, were Paul Evans and of oxblood hue. The man was without a sports coat or suit jacket, and also without a watch; but was nonetheless wearing at least two thousand dollars.

On a fucking Wednesday.

He was sizing me up as well; and for several minutes there was no conversation. He looked at his clipboard, which held the form I completed upon arrival. He grinned almost immediately. "James Joyce, huh?"

"Yes. Without question. He'd be the one."

With perfect teeth—obviously veneers—he smiled and said "Mister Pot that is undoubtedly the best response to that question I have ever seen. My name is Cecil Derrick, and it is a pleasure to meet you."

"Thank you" I said. "It's a pleasure to meet you as well. And, may I ask, what would your answer be?"

"I beg your pardon" he said as he looked at me with confusion.

"I mean…I would travel back in time to pummel that overblown, long-winded, cockeyed mick; so I am asking whom would you do the same?"

"Who? Me?" he asked. "Well, Mr. Pot, no one."

And round one goes to the good doctor. Dammit.

#

After a few minutes of banal questioning about my family and career he asked me to lie on his couch. I acquiesced, and with even my full length of seventy-two inches stretched upon the remarkable piece of leather craftsmanship, there was still enough room for the doc to sit comfortably, at the end, by my feet. He admired my Thursday boots and said he owned two pairs; which I believed--for he had no reason to lie about such a trivial thing. But I deduced those purchases were made prior to his trading-up to Paul Evans.

"I see here you were diagnosed with MDD over a decade ago, care to talk about that?' he asked.

"Nope."

"And why not? I mean, after all, MDD is a very serious condition."

"No, it's not" I snapped back.

He was writing voraciously upon his clipboard, not looking at me.

I continued: "It's not serious when everyone suffers from it."

"Everyone?" he asked, still looking at his clipboard and flipping to a new, untouched sheet of paper.

"Everyone. I mean, I'm not the only one with a dead-end job. I'm not the only one drowning in student loan debt. I can't be the only one heading into the holiday season having to choose between getting tires for his shitty car or a new iPhone for his kid."

"Please go on," said Dr. Derrick.

"No. I apologize for whining."

"Don't apologize. It's the couch's fault...it makes people open up" the doc said while cracking a faint smile. "This is your time. You strike me as a father like so many others: feeling invisible and trapped and used. And I have a pen running over with ink and a hundred blank pages in front of me. So, I beg you, for the both of us...continue."

"Well, okay doc, you asked for it...but for the record, therapy is bullshit. And I'm not the type to just talk when I know no one is listening and no one gives a shit."

"Duly noted."

"Well," I began, "you're right: invisible and used is how I feel. I am of no use to anyone unless I'm handing over a debit card or creating a monthly report at the last minute that I'll get zero credit for. I'm fucking invisible except when I squeeze my fat ass in nice pants and drive my wife and daughter to that dog-and-pony show they call their church. I mean, I'm a Christian and I love God, but he ain't showing up at this place: a for-profit, country club church if there ever was one. But I go. And even then I'm expected to hand over a check. Ain't that some shit? And fine, ok, I get it; but after a hard day's work all I want to do is lift weights then read a chapter or two in a goddamn book but I can't because I'm always behind on laundry or there's water in the basement or the grass needs cut and before I know it it's time for bed and I haven't even given my daughter a bath yet or made her sippies for the next day and I realize it's been a week since I shaved and tomorrow I have a meeting with upper management so I have to shave and then find clothes just free enough of wrinkles to make myself appear to be professional but all my nice clothes don't fit me anymore because even though I don't have time to eat I'm still gaining weight and it's not the good weight from dumbbell curls and deadlifts, no, it's the gross weight that hangs over my cheap Dockers pants but then I remind myself why even bother because no one pays the slightest bit of attention to a forty-year old no matter how much he works out and no matter how much or little his clothes cost and that his wife, ten years his junior, mind you, also has to sacrifice looking nicer to save money and God bless her for it, but this same wife can only sleep in a spooning position but she gets pissed off when his boner digs into her spine all night unbeknownst to this hapless son of a bitch and this aforementioned boner, grandiose and awe-inspiring as any slapped on mankind past present and future, is the most neglected piece on this entirely neglected son of a bitch and he unknowingly finds himself breathing but not living, going through the motions of a normal functioning male but inside is just waiting for death's sweet embrace because it is the only embrace he has to look forward to because to everyone around him he's just a fucking joke so he wonders why even try, let someone else have your spot on this earth and do the right thing and take a bath with a toaster but then he remembers his life insurance policy won't cover a suicide and the worst thing a man can do is leave his family in dire straits financially while he takes the easy way out so what to do? the guilt makes him buy a more expensive life insurance policy from the snake at church and this snake only smiles and acknowledges your presence when you're upping a policy or adding a new vehicle to a current policy and then he shakes your hand and pats your back and leans in real closely to call you 'brother' at the dog-and-pony show but he doesn't care about you he cares about getting his wife and himself back to Mexico for the second time in a year and posting pictures on fucking Facebook and they return to church from Cancun looking all tan and gorgeous and rich and as a deacon he passes and solicits the collection plate and he scoffs at your meager weekly offering of twenty-five bucks so you fold the check trying to hide the amount but it doesn't work because you're an unlucky piece of shit so the check miraculously unfolds hallelujah praise be to the Lord and not only does the snake see you only have twenty-five bucks to spare but so does the next asshole seated right beside you who proudly throws in a check for who-knows-what-amount as his wife squeezes his arm with pride and you know that asshole is getting a blowjob before the football game kicks-off and then you remember how much you hate football and then remember how much you loved baseball but another season came and went and you didn't make it to Reds game again this year and what does that make it? three or four years in a row now? yeah that sounds about right and you wonder how the NL Central fared this season and you want to take out your phone and go to mlb.com but you have to wait until there is Wi-Fi because your broke ass can't afford a phone plan with unlimited data and you look around to see other dads and deacons on their phones and probably checking mlb.com or nfl.com or xhamster.com and you're afraid to make eye contact with your wife because you're a fat fucking loser with a shitty phone plan and tits bigger than hers and you pray that you can afford to take your family to that overpriced and overcrowded mess called Disney World this year and get them all the five dollar Rice Krispie treats they can eat and you ignore the ungodly markup because the Rice Krispie treats are in the shape of a fucking fictional mouse's head and how adorable is that? and those fucking con artists get away with it as they try with increasing success to slowly ensure they never have to tolerate a blue-collar family entering their magic kingdom so you consider taking a second job but your wife says no because for all your shortcomings you are a decent husband and father and they would miss you at home on nights and weekends so you grin and bear it and do great work at your shitty job in hopes your boss dies or retires so you can move up the ladder and make a little more money but then you call yourself a piece of shit for hoping your boss dies because David has been great to you and come Monday you won't look him in the eye because you feel bad and you remember that you are a lowly workaday asshole and your lot in life is to be faceless yet productive and accountable so you decide to sell your old baseball cards and first-edition novels because someone somewhere in this shitty town needs a Willie Stargell rookie card so you post these items online and they sit there and sit there until you finally slash the prices by half which gives you just enough money for three tee shirts at Disney and you hate yourself because those cards and those books were going to be given to your daughter as a way of remembering you when you finally die but now they're gone so you track down the buyer and buy them back at twenty percent more than you sold them and the realization that you were born a loser and will always be a loser really sinks in and you're ashamed of yourself so you vow to spend even more time with your wife and daughter and your daughter wants to play because she's just three years old and you get on the floor and let her ride your back like you're a pony but your forty-year-old knees scream whatthebloodyhell! and you roll on your side in agony so your daughter goes back to playing on her tablet and forgetting that you exist at all because you don't because you are simply a nonentity, a skeptical and insecure nonentity and everyone knows it you feel embarrassed for even trying and because you're embarrassed and sad your wife and your co-workers think you should get help and they look for professional help and they say 'spare no expense' and they say 'just get better' because they love you for some reason and for some reason you hate yourself and so you give in and you find a place that accepts your shitty insurance and you take the morning off from work and you're vague to your boss about why you need the morning off; you say 'appointment' and hope he takes that to mean a real doctor visit and not a shrink because God forbid people know you're human and you feel overwhelmed and that you hate Disney and you hate being broke and tired and invisible so you stick to your appointment and you drive to the richest part of town in your nicest clothes and you hope you can maintain the façade of control long enough to get through the hour without the shrink admitting the good and proper thing to do is to throw yourself off of Carew Tower and the sooner the better so you spill your guts because let's face it you're never going to see this rich asshole again and sit on his eight thousand dollar couch again and so you don't care what he writes in his little notepad with his little Montblanc fountain pen you're just happy to be out of the office for a little bit and that your wife agreed to take your daughter to dance class herself tonight freeing-up enough time for you to read a chapter of *Ulysses* by James fuckin' Joyce and get caught up on laundry and you smile because it's the best day you've had in a long time."

It was at that moment I lifted my head to see if Dr. Derrick was still there. He was. He was tapping his pen on his notepad with his right hand, and his left was pinching the bridge of his nose. The doctor's stomach growled. I sat quietly.

"You know," he began, "some policies actually *do* cover suicide."

Red

Red was never one to keep a place tidy. Whether it was his apartment or his van, the place was a mess. It's not that he was a lazy person; in fact, quite the opposite was true. He just, I guess one could say, prioritized most things above cleanliness.

Following the suicide, his little brother JD was tasked with the cleaning of Red's home and storage facility. In most families it was customary for the eldest children to oversee the correcting of the messes the younger ones made; but, that was never the case in the Bertrand household. JD was the more mature of the two, though being Red's junior by two years. And as such, JD was bequeathed the responsibility of looking after his big brother. He hated it, Red did, but…you know, that's life.

His most recent, and final, place of residence (prior to the Ricker-White Memorial Gardens, I mean) was a cheaply-constructed duplex built in the late-eighties in an area of West Chester that seemingly missed out on the rest of the township's prosperity. His eleven-hundred square feet was on the east side of the house, which was a waste considering he had never seen a sunrise in his life. He would have been much better-suited occupying the identical half of the house on the other side of the drywall adjacent to him. Sunsets were preferable to Red.

Red's band had been back home from their latest tour –for lack of a better word—for just nine days before he shot himself. One would think in those nine days of self-imposed isolation and self-reflection that it would occur to him to tidy the place up a bit. To scrub the toilet or do the dishes or pick up his underwear that littered the bedroom, for example. But he did not. When his grim pensiveness got the better of him he was of no use to himself or to anyone. And unfortunately these instances occurred with more frequency the last few years of his life. He swore to JD and to his mother that he was taking his prescribed medications with the suggested regularity; however, JD found no prescription pill bottles in the apartment. The remnants of medicine found were of a recreational nature.

Few photographs were in the home. Just two on the refrigerator door, to be precise. One was of JD and Red hovering above John Fante's grave during a trip to Malibu four years' prior; the other picture was of Red's band *Rust & Stardust* sharing beers with Chino Moreno inside the filthy toilet of whatever club or bar the two acts were playing that night. Their latest tour was the same ten venues in the same eight cities as the previous tour.

JD has just finished the last of Red's dirty dishes and began filling yet another large garbage bag full of the refuse when it finally hit him: the knowledge—the certitude--that his brother was gone. Red was truly and irreversibly done for. He would never again regale his little brother with stories from the road; even if the road just meant a hundred-mile radius. No more laughing about sharting himself onstage; no horror stories about syphilitic groupies or happening upon his bass player balls-deep in one; no late night e-mails with potential song lyrics, asking JD for a thumbs-up or thumbs-down. JD tried to put that out of mind and shift his emotion to anger as he soaked sponges in the cracked blue bucket before lowering to his tired knees. Anger was easier than sadness. So bitterness and anger would be his ally as he cleaned up the dried blood on the wall, floor, and even the ceiling.

Hours passed before JD looked back to admire his handiwork, just as the sun was setting. He stepped out the backdoor and on to the deck to have a smoke. He was tired, and he looked forward to the following day (Sunday) of sleeping in late and listening to his brother's music on repeat. So tired he was that he failed to notice he was not alone.

"Why'd he do it?"

The voice, sweet as it was, startled JD, and he dropped his cigarette between two cracks in the wooden deck. On the other half of the deck, separated by a waist-high wooden partition, was a young boy. He looked to be about ten years old, deduced JD; though he was never good at guessing ages.

"I'm sorry?"

"Red. Why'd he do it? Was he sad?"

JD looked the kid in the eyes and realized that he did not have an answer. "Well, I really don't know. I wish I knew, but I just don't."

"He didn't leave a note or nothin'? That's weird; me and my mom would see him writing out here on the deck all the time. So we figured he at least left a note." The young man had his skinny and befreckled arms folded on the partition, his chin resting on them.

"No. No note." JD then walked over to the boy and extended his hand. "JD Bertrand. I'm Red's brother."

"Jared," the boy said accepting JD's hand. "Jared Bradley. Most people call me Jay."

"Well, Jay, it's pleasure to meet you. Did you know my brother pretty well?"

"Kinda, I guess. I've lived here my whole life. And he moved in a few years back. My mom helped him carry some stuff in. And she helped him pick out curtains and stuff. He was always nice to us. Mom said he was a rock star, but he never had no crazy parties or nothin' like that. He even helped me with my math homework a couple times."

"Oh yeah? Well that was nice of him. He was always good at math."

Both of them stood where they were; both looking down at their feet. JD usually looked at such silence as the perfect opportunity to end a conversation and subsequently leave; but, for some reason, he didn't mind talking to Jay.

"He killed our cat, you know."

"He what now?" asked JD with a raised eyebrow.

"Yep. When he…you know…*did it*. When he pulled the trigger on that big old shotgun Mom said some of the buckshot or whatever came through the walls and hit our cat, who was sleeping at the time, on the back of our couch. Some of it caught him in the side. He didn't die right away. We took him to the vet, and the vet said we need to put him down. So we did. Mom was ticked. She loved that couch. Now it has holes in it."

"Yeah, I bet she was pretty upset. Tell her I'm sorry." replied JD.

The kid shrugged his shoulders. "I'm just sorry he was so sad."

"Don't be sorry. It was his fault."

"What do you mean?"

"I mean, and I don't mean to besmirch the dead here, but Red didn't realize that his actions hurt others, too."

"Like my cat?"

"Yes. Your cat; your mom; your couch; you. I don't think he would have done it then if he knew that an animal would get hurt. Or if he knew your mom would be upset."

"I guess you're right. He didn't seem like the type to hurt anybody."

"He wasn't," confirmed JD. "He was a vegetarian."

"What's that?"

"It means he didn't eat meat."

"Oh," said Jay. "That's weird."

"Yeah, I guess so."

By now the sun was setting and evening's chill bit their skin. JD, in a tee shirt and nothing on his arms, began rubbing his shoulders hoping to induce some warmth. Jay remained in the same position as before, though also just in a tee.

"So...why'd he do it?"

"Because he was crazy, kid. Because he was selfish and dumb and just plain crazy."

Jay lifted his head to better see JD. He wanted to understand.

"It was his thirtieth birthday" continued JD. "And he thought if he hadn't made it as a rock-n-roll legend by thirty he was never going to. So he sat his sorry, skinny ass against a wall, placed his favorite books around him, and put both barrels of our dad's antique shotgun in his mouth. He pulled the trigger and killed your cat and ruined my Saturday."

For the first time since he heard the news, JD could feel hot tears filling his eyes. They welled-up, then they rolled down his cheeks. He hated feeling sad; being angry was infinitely easier. Sadness is hard work.

There was an extended period of silence. Neither knew what to say next; or if even there was anything left to say at all. JD shuffled his feet and stared at the crack in the deck that stole the cigarette he desperately longed for at that moment. He needed a smoke, or a good cry; or something to punch.

"Was it the Russians?"

"What?" JD asked, obviously confused. He turned his body to face Jay, in hopes of better understanding the question.

"His favorite books. The ones he placed around himself. He told me about 'em: The Russians. Like Nakobov, or somethin' like that; and Leo Toystory. He liked Toystory's short stories, he told me."

JD couldn't help but to smile and laugh a little. "Yep. Nakobov and Toystory are the best."

They smiled at one another and watched the heavens steal from them the day's last light.

CPSIA information can be obtained
at www.ICGtesting.com
Printed in the USA
LVHW090445300920
667463LV00004B/1416